C0-GEC-802

Rhiann's Rescue
F Irw
T54895

Mediapolis Public Library

pet rescue workers
ıgh fostering, vol-
my heroes!

DATE DUE

MAY 1 1 2022			

PRINTE

DISCARDED

Help us Rate this book...
Put your initials on the
Left side and your rating
on the right side.
1 = Didn't care for
2 = It was O.K.
3 = It was great

DV ______ 1 2 3
______ 1 2 3
______ 1 2 3
______ 1 2 3
______ 1 2 3
______ 1 2 3
______ 1 2 3
______ 1 2 3
______ 1 2 3
______ 1 2 3
______ 1 2 3
______ 1 2 3
______ 1 2 3
______ 1 2 3
______ 1 2 3

MEDIAPOLIS PUBLIC LIBRARY
128 N. ORCHARD ST.
PO BOX 39
MEDIAPOLIS, IA 52637

Chapter 1

Rhiann Kelly sat in the bay window, her knees pulled up near her chin. Steamers of apricot, peach, and tangerine flooded the eastern sky, although many of Spokane's high-rise condos and commercial buildings blocked her view. Her hand surrounded a steaming cup of coffee and a crackling fire blazed in the living room hearth, helping thwart the chill from the late December day.

She sighed as she gazed at the dawn.

"Why do I do this to myself?" Rhiann spoke softly to herself. "Happens every time."

Her eyes left the outdoors, which not only unveiled the dawn sky, but also revealed splashes of green, red, blue, and white lights surrounding roofs and wrapped around porch poles in her neighborhood. Christmas hovered in the community's rearview mirror; however, a recent blast of snow kept many homes still decorated for the holiday. New Year's Eve loomed on the horizon. Rhiann sighed with relief that she hadn't agreed to the date set-up with one of her grandmother's friends for that night.

No, that too, was in the rearview mirror, and for that she was grateful.

"That was another disaster," she mumbled.

The blind date she had last night went as well as the one she'd agreed to six months ago – horribly – and resurrected memories of *him*. Brandon, the man she had planned to marry more than a decade ago.

"I'm getting too old for this," Rhiann muttered as she continued staring at the awakening day.

She took a sip of coffee and continued her perusal of the morning sky. One by one, stars faded, replaced by twinges of pastel clouds hanging by tendrils like spider webbing.

She took a deep breath and then whispered on the exhale, "Enough is enough. No more dates. I don't care which of Grams' friend's grandsons those old ladies conspire to set me up with. It's pets and writing for me ... forever."

Just then, Poppy, the longhaired Seal point Persian she and Grams adopted nearly twelve years ago , hopped onto the window seat, and rubbed her cheek against Rhiann's feet. The 40-year-old woman smiled as the purring cat stretched toward her.

"Hey, there, sweet girl," Rhiann said, scratching Poppy's cream-colored chin. "The single life has been good for you, and it will continue to be good for me, right?"

As she tickled the cat's chin, Rhiann fixed her gaze upon the dimly lit living room. The Christmas tree she and Grams had chosen two weeks ago remained erect in the northwestern corner of the room. White lights sparkled like stars upon the dark green fir branches. This Pacific Northwest conifer had been the Christmas tree of choice since her teenage years.

"Friendly fir," her grandfather had always reminded her when time came to select a holiday tree. She smiled as she recalled his baritone voice.

Grams' decorations adorned the mighty conifer, that not only reached nearly six feet tall, but was full and round, just as her grandmother liked. Ornaments from early years of marriage between her grandparents as well as many from Rhiann's childhood before her parents' passing trimmed the needled branches while white lights and red garland encircled the fir.

The peaceful surroundings helped still Rhiann's edginess.

"We do create a fine Currier and Ives holiday setting, don't we, Miss Poppy?"

The cat leaned toward her and massaged Rhiann's face with her own, as if in agreement. The woman chuckled and then caressed the top of Poppy's head, running her fingers between the feline's ears. "You're up early this morning, sweet girl."

"So are you," came Grams' low voice.

Rhiann glanced up. She watched as her silver and black-haired 79-year-old grandmother ambled down the stairs. Rhiann gave Poppy another soft stroke under the chin and then swung her legs off the window seat.

"Mornin', Grams. Coffee's hot."

"Wonderful. I could use a cup."

Rhiann hurried into the kitchen. She reached for Grams' favorite coffee mug, the hand-painted one Grandpops had special-ordered for Grams' 70th birthday. Poppy's portrait stared back at Rhiann. She smiled and ran a finger across the ceramic cup. She glanced at the brown-framed photo hanging above the yellow-gingham curtained kitchen window. The image of her grandparents at their orchard reflected. Rhiann sighed and then turned back to the blue and white tiled counter. She removed the glass carafe from the coffee maker and filled Grams' mug with the hot liquid. She walked into the adjacent dining area and watched her grandmother bestow affection on Poppy. Rhiann smiled again. She set the cup of coffee on the oak dining table as Grams walked into the room. Rhiann pulled a chair out for her, and Grams gave her granddaughter a kiss on the cheek and a quick smile.

"So, why up so early on a Saturday morning?" the older woman inquired as she sat down.

"I have a transport later, remember?"

Grams sipped her coffee and then nodded. "But like you said – later. Out with it."

Rhiann sighed and pulled out a chair. "No more blind dates, Grams – no fixing me up with single grandsons of your friends."

"That bad, uh?"

Rhiann looked at the woman she'd admired for so many years. "First, class A BORING, and secondly, came on like a hormone-crazed teenager. I'm glad I had my own car."

Grams shook her head. "I'm sorry, dear. You'd think a 40-year-old would have better sense."

"I don't think men in general have much sense, Grams."

The older woman chuckled. "Only if they've been married 40 years or more – to the same woman."

Rhiann smiled. "That doesn't happen much these days."

"No, it certainly doesn't."

Both women sipped their coffee.

"So, tell me again about this transport," Grams prompted.

"I pick the dog up at 11:30 and take it to Kellogg. Rachel, the transporter from Missoula meets me and takes the dog back with her."

"Too bad you're not able to go all the way to Missoula – you could pick up some property information."

Rhiann gave her grandmother a determined look. "Grams, we're not moving to Montana. This is our home, at least most of the year."

Grams sighed. "I know. I just keep wishing we could ..."

"We can't and that's that. The trips to Arizona are hard enough on you. In fact, I'm thinking we should cancel this year ...."

"No!" The admonishment startled Rhiann. Grams sighed. "I'm sorry for my harsh tone. Our annual trip south is the one thing I have to look forward to, and I'm not giving that up. Not yet at least."

Rhiann drank more of her coffee. "Okay, Grams, I understand. It's just that your heart hasn't been as good this year, and the doctor said you need to take it easy. A week's drive to Arizona isn't taking it easy."

"You may be right, but like I said, I look forward to getting away from this blasted winter, and that does my heart good."

Rhiann smiled. "Well, I must admit, I look forward to the sunshine and colorful cactus, too."

Grams smiled back. "And you have that rescue that wants you again this year."

"And you know I like that, too!"

Silence fell between them for a few moments. Grams' next statement startled Rhiann.

"I take it you've been thinking about Brandon again." Rhiann looked at her. "It's about that time of year."

Rhiann sighed. "I can't hide anything from you, can I?" Grams shook her head. "I guess when the love of your life turns his back on you, even years later the hurt is just like a hornet's sting."

"I'm sorry, sweetie. You gave up your whole life for your grandpops and me..."

Rhiann reached over and patted her grandmother's hand. "The two of you did the same for me and Erin when we were kids. There was never any doubt I'd be here when you needed me. We've talked about this before."

"Still, the older I get and knowing you don't date that much ..."

Rhiann shook her head. "No more of that. I have you, you have me, and we both have Poppy. We're our own little family, and that's just fine with me."

Her grandmother nodded, took another drink from her coffee mug, and then said. "Speaking of your sister, Erin, I saw in the paper last night that the fellow she went to prom with? Michael Jacobs, the vet? He just received some big award for his veterinary practice in Seattle."

"I don't think I remember him," Rhiann commented.

"You don't? Oh, I still do. Sweet kid! I always wished they would have reconnected."

"Erin and Daniel are a good match, and she's happy. I don't think some guy from senior prom has likely ever crossed her mind."

"Unlike you with Brandon."

Like fast-forwarding through a movie, Rhiann recalled the last time she saw the man she had planned to marry. His words had been as abrupt and unexpected as if he'd slapped her face.

"What do you mean, 'move to Washington?' My life, my career is here in Boise. So is yours."

"But I'm their only relative able to take care of them!"

"You have a sister – let her do it."

"Brandon, you know Erin has a family and a husband who's in the Air Force. She can't just drop everything and go to the farm."

"Neither can you – our life is here, together. We've been talking marriage for a month, as soon as I finish at the law enforcement academy."

"We can still do that. We can still get married when you're done," she had tried to reason with him. "There are plenty of law enforcement jobs in and around the Spokane area. I've checked. City police, sheriff's office ..."

"What?! You checked?! So, you just assumed I'd uproot myself and go so you can take care of your grandparents? My family's here, my parents, my brother and sister ..."

Anger welled up in Rhiann. "Well, my family is near Spokane! You know good and well that Grams and Grandpops raised Erin and me after our parents died. I owe them! Now that his health is declining, I'm needed ..."

"What about my needs, Rhiann? I don't owe your grandparents anything, and I'm not going!" Brandon had taken a deep breath and stared at her. "You choose, Rhiann – me and Boise or your grandparents in Washington."

She made her choice, and now, after another awful date, here she sat.

I have a good life with Grams, her brain reasoned. *I'm a pretty successful freelance writer, and I help rescue animals.*

Her beloved elder interrupted her thoughts. "Rhiann? Dear? Are you okay?"

The auburn-haired woman looked at her grandmother and nodded. "Yes. Just lost in thought for a few moments." She sipped her coffee. "I love that picture of you and Grandpops we have in the kitchen. I miss the farm, the orchard, at times."

Grams nodded. "Me, too. I supposed that's a reason I push for us to move to Montana. I'm growing weary of the city. I'd rather spend my final years in a rural area again."

Rhiann reached for her grandmother's hand and took it into her own.

"You know that's not practical," she said in a gentle voice. "That's why we moved into Spokane – to be closer to medical services. We needed to for Grandpops and we need to for you. Heck, even for me!"

"Fresh air does a body good," Grams responded. "My parents stayed on the homestead all of their lives. I think being in the city isn't that great for you either."

Grams patted her hand.

Rhiann shrugged. "It's more like the dreary weather. That cold snap and snow we had earlier this week didn't do my mood much good. The blind date last night didn't help either." She pasted on a smile and again squeezed her grandmother's hand. "But we had a lovely Christmas with Eleanor and her daughter, and I know Grandpops would have approved of the tree we chose this year."

Both women glanced at the fir for a moment.

"Your grandfather taught you well on how to pick out a lovely Christmas tree," Grams said in a quiet voice. "I always miss him most this time of year." She looked at Rhiann. "Kind of like you and Brandon."

Rhiann stood and took her coffee cup to the sink. Poppy sauntered from the living room and rubbed against the woman's legs. Rhiann picked up the affectionate cat and rubbed her cheek on top of the kitty's head.

"Yeah, well, if I hadn't gone on that date last night, and if the guy hadn't of been such a dolt ..." She shrugged, with nonchalance and to rid herself of the doldrums.

"Some Arizona sunshine and warmth will do us both good, and the pet rescue work will shake these blahs quick enough." Isn't that right, Poppy?"

She hugged the cat and then set her down. "Speaking of rescue, I better hit the shower and get ready for my drive today. How about I fix us some breakfast after I let some hot water wake me up a bit more?"

Rhiann walked toward her grandmother, still sitting at the table.

"Sounds good, honey. Would you grab my tablet from the lamp table near my chair? I have a crossword puzzle I can try to finish before breakfast." Rhiann stepped away. "Oh, did you hear anything on that article you submitted *to Big Sky Magazine*? The one about the cranes and the moose?"

"No, not yet. I don't expect an answer for another week or two. Everybody's still getting back from their holiday."

She walked into the living room, picked up the electronic tablet she'd given to her grandmother as a Christmas present, and brought it to the older woman.

"Here you go, Grams. You've become really good at that thing, by the way." She kissed her grandmother's cheek. "I'll be down in about thirty minutes."

"Take your time. As the old musical goes, 'Wash that man right outta your hair!"

After sharing a chuckle, Rhiann kissed her grandmother's cheek and left the room, walking up the stairs to her bedroom.

Chapter 2

Driving Interstate 90 between Spokane, Washington and Coeur de Alene, Idaho two hours later, Rhiann allowed the open road to continue the work her grandmother suggested. The cobalt sky and sparkling sunshine lifted her spirits, helping her release thoughts of Brandon and last night's miserable date. The dog stationed in the booster seat strapped to her Toyota RAV's backseat also helped.

Rhiann glanced in the rearview mirror to peek in the back seat. The black cocker spaniel, nose pressed to the back window, watched the world zip by and appeared fascinated at the speed by which the roadway, the brown grasses and shrubs, and the electrical poles along the highway passed by his eyes. Rhiann smiled. She never tired at the joy and wonder that illuminated from the four-footed passengers she transported for various animal rescue organizations.

As the highway stretched in front of her, Rhiann reflected upon her passion for pets. She recalled the menagerie of animals she and her sister experienced, thanks to parents, and later grandparents, who allowed the siblings to experience, even take in different types of creatures. On Grams' and Grandpops' small farm, where the girls came to live during their late teen years after the death of their parents, they a collection of barnyard animals, including sheep, goats, cows, and horses. Thanks to Grams' continual love of learning, the women began making their own butter, cheese, soap, and lotions, selling the soaps and lotions at fairs and other events and online. College detoured such entrepreneurial endeavors, but she had volunteered at the Boise animal shelter, which helped feed her passion.

Rhiann's memories of those days brought warmth and smiles whenever she recalled them – such as now. Transporting dogs for rescue groups brought the same warmth and smile, although often the animals' stories carried sad beginnings.

She again glanced in the rearview mirror. The cocker had settled into his seat. Eyes closed and head propped against the left side of the black padded bar, he appeared asleep. She hoped he'd settle just as comfortably with the new family that awaited him in Montana, and she hoped the dog would continue riding well to Missoula, another three hours' drive east. Rhiann felt gratitude for Rachel, the next transporter, who was driving from her Missoula home to meet her and then driving back. Rhiann recalled her discussion last week when Rachel contacted her about the transport.

"I prefer not to take long trips anymore because of my grandmother's health," she had told Rachel. "Driving to Missoula and back would be an all-day deal and I just don't want to be gone that long right now."

"No worries. If you can get the dog to Kellogg, I'll meet you there."

"Thanks, Rachel. That I can do."

Rhiann glanced at the pup in the back seat again. "If you think you're tired now, little guy, I wonder how you'll feel in about four hours?" she mused aloud.

The indigo waters of Lake Coeur de Alene came into view, and Rhiann lifted her foot from the RAV's accelerator pedal. As the vehicle slowed, she again glanced in the mirrors, first right, then left, and then rearview.

Her eyes caught the gleam of another vehicle's windshield. A black pickup truck whose driver obviously disregarded the slower in-town speed limit barreled forward. The interstate sliced through town, but due to heavier traffic and recreational vehicles going to and coming from the large lake within the community, the speed limit decreased from 70 to 50. Highway signs warned drivers of the new, slower speed. Rhiann recognized the approaching truck traveled more than that as it moved closer to her bumper.

"He'll get over," she murmured as she glanced forward again.

Her certainty waned as she again looked at her mirrors. She pressed the accelerator again to move her vehicle ahead quicker. The RAV choked, causing a delay. The driver behind Rhiann realized the truck's approach was too fast for the front wheels turned left, but not before the pickup's front bumper clipped the RAV's back one. As her vehicle began to spin, Rhiann eased off the accelerator and maneuvered the steering wheel as her father and grandfather taught her. Slushy conditions caused the RAV to do an extra spin.

"Damn!" Rhiann muttered.

She heard the pup in the backseat whine, but she focused her attention on keeping the SUV upright. She pumped the brakes and whipped her head to check traffic conditions. Fortunately, people had pulled their cars to the shoulder, giving her vehicle room as it skidded. The SUV bounced once off the right guardrail, and Rhiann heard the crunch of her vehicle's front bumper. She shook her head at the sound but then concentrated on regaining control and easing the RAV to a stop along the right shoulder. After setting the vehicle's emergency flashers, she also set the brake.

Rhiann looked back and, to her relief, the cocker spaniel was still securely stationed in his booster seat. She reached her arm backward and scratched the dog's head. Emergency sirens sounded from behind. Rhiann looked in the rearview mirror again. In the distance, she caught the flickering blue and red lights of a law enforcement vehicle. She also noticed the black truck that caused the accident sat in the median separating the east and west-bound lanes of I-90. The vehicle was upright and the driver was out of the truck, walking around the damaged vehicle.

Rhiann sighed and leaned her head on the steering wheel. She took several deep breaths before picking up her cell phone, holstered in a black stand affixed to the dash. As a highway patrol vehicle pulled in behind her RAV and another pulled onto the shoulder of the east bound lane, Rhiann did a speed dial to the transporter with whom she was to rendezvous.

"Rachel, this is Rhiann. I won't be meeting you in Kellogg; I've been in an accident. I'm okay and Coal, the dog, is all right. My vehicle, however, is not. I need you to come to Coeur de Alene. Call me when you get this message."

Rhiann hung up and pushed the window button as the officer walked up. Bundled in a brown leather jacket with the Idaho Highway Patrol insignia branding the coat, an image of Brandon flashed through her brain. Rhiann shook her head as if to vanquish the image.

Upon reaching Rhiann's door, the man titled his hat back.

"Are you okay? Do you need an ambulance?"

"No, officer, I'm all right." She put a thumb through her seatbelt. "Thanks to this."

He nodded. "Good for you." He glanced in the back seat. "Good thing you strapped your four-footed friend in as well. I'll need to take your statement, but first may I see your driver's license and registration?"

"Yes, sir. The registration is in the glove box and my driver's license is in my purse in the passenger's seat."

He nodded and watched her reach for the information he requested, keeping his right hand on his holstered gun. After Rhiann collected the documents, she handed them to the officer. He glanced over them and then cocked his right eyebrow. Looking at Rhiann again, he said, "I know you."

"Really? I'm not sure I know you."

He unzipped his burley coat and widened the fabric, showing his name plate. Rhiann read "R. Hastings."

"Randall, Randy Hastings. I attended the academy with Brandon."

Rhiann's eyes widened. "Randy! My gosh! It's been an awfully long time."

He grinned. "That it has." He looked at her car registration again. "Washington. Isn't Brandon still with the Boise district? I saw him at a training in McCall last summer."

Rhiann's eyes fell for a moment. She looked back up and said in a quiet voice, "Brandon and I aren't together. Haven't been for nearly a decade."

"Well, dang! I'd never have thought ... The only thing he talked about more than being in law enforcement back then was you. Rhiann – his classy, beautiful Irish lass."

Rhiann looked away and bit her lip. "Well, he loved law enforcement more than this bonny lass."

Her phone rang. She glanced at the screen and recognized the number of the Montana transporter.

"I need to get this – it involves the dog."

He nodded, and she picked up the call.

"Hey, Rachel." She paused. "Yeah, yeah, I'm fine, so is Coal. Sorry to make you drive farther, but I'll be dealing with this accident for a while." Another pause. "Great, thanks. I'll text you where I'll be so you can pick him up. Thanks again."

She clicked off and looked at the officer. "I transport dogs for rescue. This one's going to Missoula." She nodded to the back of the RAV. "Can you contact a tow truck for me?"

"Already done," Officer Hastings said. "Why don't you meet me back at the cruiser and we'll get started on your statement?"

Rhiann nodded and pushed the button to raise the window.

"I'll be glad for the New Year, and man, I can't wait to get to Arizona!" she muttered.

Chapter 3

Three weeks later, as she lounged near the pool at The Magnifico Resort near Phoenix, Rhiann held a small laptop on her knees. Adobe villas surrounded the manicured lawns brimming with blooming roses and tall palm trees. Braided lights roped around fences, including the three-foot-tall black iron fencing that enclosed the oval pool and large lounging area.

Within several yards of the resort loomed rolling hills of desert landscape, including saguaro, barrel, prickly pear, and other cactus, many about to bloom. The 75-degree temperature warmed her skin as Rhiann relished the sunny sky while wearing her one-piece aqua-colored bathing suit with a white and cyan covering. She read the email she had received.

"Hi, Rhiann – I'm delighted to tell you that your story, 'Moose Prance While Sandhills Dance: My Yellowstone Experience,' has been accepted for the summer issue of *Big Sky Magazine*. Congratulations! I'll be working with you during the next two months to edit the article for publication. You will receive $500 compensation, more with photos (which I believe you told me you have). I'll send a contract with greater details in the next day or two and ask you to return a signed copy to me within one week. Thanks for your submission, and I look forward to working with you. If you have ideas for upcoming issues, please let me know. We are excited to work with you on your submitted story and other possible future articles. Sincerely, Etta Grace Johannsen – Managing Editor, *Big Sky Magazine.*"

A grin spread across Rhiann's face.

"Dang, I love what I do!"

"That's always a good thing, I believe."

The deep masculine voice caused Rhiann to jerk her head. Her green eyes locked on the suntanned face of a man in his mid-40s, onyx eyes shining and full lips smiling. Rhiann startled.

"Oh! I didn't hear anyone walk up."

"Attributes of great walking shoes."

He extended a leg to show off blue canvas boat loafers. Smile still on his face, the man asked, "So what do you do that makes you love your work?"

Rhiann closed the laptop. "I'm a writer."

"Really? Awesome! I'm a nature photographer and art gallery owner." He extended his hand. "Elias Griffin."

She shook his hand. "Rhiann Kelly."

"Rhiann? A unique, beautiful name."

"Elias – that's a name a person doesn't often hear."

He nodded. "Technically, I'm Elias Griffin the third. However, since my father and grandfather have already passed on, I dropped the more formal version."

"I'm sorry they've passed. So have mine."

"And I'm sorry for your loss, Miss Kelly – or is it Mrs.?"

"You were right the first time," Rhiann responded, maintaining her smile.

He bowed slightly. "Miss Kelly." He nodded toward a chair nearby. "Would you mind if I sit for a few moments?"

Rhiann shook her head and responded, "No, please. Have a seat."

"Thank you."

He chose the chair closest to her. Rhiann sat up straight and placed her laptop in a blue, green, and yellow tote bag. She looked at her visitor. Dressed in a short-sleeved green polo shirt and khaki kicker-style pants, the chocolate brown-haired man appeared more dressed for the golf course than the pool. She pondered his presence in this 55-and-older community. Being Grams' caregiver allowed Rhiann to stay here.

"So, do you have family here, Mr. Griffin?" He gave her a quizzical look. "You just don't seem to fit the required age group."

He smiled. "Neither do you, Miss Kelly."

"I take care of my grandmother, so when we come here during the winter, I can stay with her."

"My mother is giving snowbirding a try for the first time. She came down the first of the year. I have a home in Mesa with an art gallery in downtown Phoenix and one in Tucson. I visit Mother whenever I can."

"I imagine owning galleries in two cities keeps you busy."

He nodded. "But I take a few mornings a week and Sundays to play golf with my mother. That's one of the reasons she chose this place – the golf course as well as the swimming pool. Plus, being in Cave Creek, it's a good stop after I've spent time at the gallery in Tucson, so I'm able to see her before going home." He indicated his attire. "This was a golf day."

"I gathered," she said with a smile. "How is she liking her stay so far?"

"She's greatly enjoying it. She's been tiring of winter for the past few years, so we made plans for her to come down and be near me this year. Plus, my sister lives in El Paso. Mom will visit my sister in a few weeks."

"Where does your mother live the rest of the year?"

"Montana. Missoula, Montana." Rhiann stared at him. "What? Don't tell me that's where you and your grandmother live?"

Rhiann shook her head, a large smile on her face. "No, but it's an area Grams may want to live. We're discussing a move to Montana – we currently live in Spokane – but Grams was raised in Montana and she wants to return."

He smiled. "What a sweet nickname for your grandmother. Sounds as if you are close."

Rhiann nodded. "We are. I've been her caregiver for nearly fifteen years. Technically, I came to live with her and my grandfather when he took ill, but she's needed my help since then, so ..." Her voice trailed off.

"I understand. How long have the two of you been coming to Arizona?"

"This is our seventh year." She smiled. "Seems like every year we come down just a little bit earlier. We had a snowstorm and major cold snap right around Christmas, so we headed out the week after New Year's."

He smiled. "My mother arrived just last week. She made it through two snowstorms. She had intended to wait until the first of February, but I was able to get her in here at the Magnifico a few weeks early."

Rhiann glanced around. "It is a lovely place. This is our fifth year here. Once we found it, we just continued reserving it for our winter's stay." She looked at Elias again. "Does your mother live right in Missoula or on the outskirts? Frenchtown? Lolo?"

Elias chuckled. "You know the area."

She nodded. "I have a friend who lives near Fort Missoula."

"I think my mother and your grandmother should meet, and I'm sure my mother would like to meet you as well. Tell you what – it's almost lunchtime. How about I treat you ladies to lunch at Del Ray's restaurant here at the Magnifico?"

"Lunch would be wonderful, but you don't need to pay for me and Grams."

"Nonsense, I insist. I'd like to hear more about your writing."

"And I'd enjoy learning more about your galleries. Grams and I enjoy exploring, and art galleries are always on our list."

He gave her a dazzling smile. "Well, if you haven't visited the two of mine, I'd love for you to stop by sometime. I bring in delightful artists nearly every weekend, and I carry a great selection of paintings and pottery. Most are southwest artisans, including some from the Hopi, Navaho, and Apache tribes."

Rhiann smiled back. "Sounds lovely."

He stood. "I'll find my mother and meet you and your grandmother at the restaurant in about twenty minutes."

She nodded. "We'll be there."

Rhiann watched him walk away and bit her lower lip. Her brain scolded, *Not so fast, Rhiann. Remember how the male species hurts and takes advantage.*

She swung her legs off the lounger, gathered her tote bag, and walked toward Grams' cottage.

Chapter 4

A few hours later, Rhiann drove her new RAV 4 along the side roads of Cave Creek, her grandmother in the passenger's seat.

"Such a nice woman, that Helen Griffin!" Grams said. "I'm so glad Elias walked over to talk with you. I believe I've made a new friend."

"I think you have, too, and I'm grateful she's willing to let me interview her for the story I plan to pitch to *Big Sky Magazine.*"

"What an incredible idea – blending the 'migration' of northerners to the southwest with the migration of sandhill cranes in the fall. Clever, my dear, very clever!"

"Thanks. I hope the editor likes the idea. I think it's unique."

"It certainly is. You get that creativeness from your mother's side. She was a beautiful interior designer and her business was gaining ground, " Grams shook her head. "We all lost so much that day your parents died."

Rhiann reached over and squeezed her grandmother's hand. After a few moments of silence, she asked, "Did his mother seem interested in joining some of the groups you're part of at the resort?"

"Bridge and watercolors yes, knitting no," Grams replied.

"The painting doesn't surprise me with her son owning two art galleries."

"You and Elias seemed engrossed in conversation a few times."

"He's fascinating, I must say. Starting his business from ground-level after losing his government job due to downsizing – I'd say he's courageous."

"So are you, honey. Look at all you've done in the past fifteen years."

"I'm doing what I love, but I don't get rich off my writing. Sounds as though Elias has done very well for himself."

"Well, the market is right and ripe down here. You're both doing something you love, and you do well enough. Plus you get to do what else you love – rescue animals."

"That's because you don't charge me rent."

She smiled at her grandmother as she pulled into the grocery store parking lot . After selecting a space, she set the RAV's parking brake and reached over to pat the older woman's knee.

"Well, you do take care of me," Grams said. "I likely couldn't live at home if it weren't for you. Speaking of home, I liked a lot of what I heard his mother, Helen, say about Missoula. Nice community, things for seniors, open space, and nature trails for you, plus a lot of nature-related groups, which might be helpful for your writing career. And good healthcare organizations."

Rhiann nodded. "I liked what I heard, too, especially if that's what you're set on doing. Some of the rescue groups I've worked with are based in Montana, as you know, so networking in that state would be fairly easy, I'd think."

"Let's spend some time looking online when we get back."

Rhiann looked at her grandmother. "Are you sure you really want to pursue this, Grams?"

The white-haired woman nodded. "It won't be the old homestead, but that's just a pipe dream anyway. But we could visit the area sometime. I want to return to my home-state, dear."

Rhiann clasped her grandmother's hand. "Okay, we'll start looking online after I get back from my transport tomorrow. I'm glad you and Helen will have the painting class together in the morning. I have to leave around ten since I need to drive to Flagstaff and back."

"Small dogs this trip, didn't you say?"

Rhiann nodded. "Their owner passed away and the family put them in the shelter. I get to bring them to Jennifer's rescue in Scottsdale."

"You should take some time and go shopping while you're there. Visit Old Town. We haven't done that the last few winters we've been down here."

Rhiann smiled and removed her hand from her grandmother's grasp. "Too many dog rescues and transports then. Besides, you know I'm not much of a shopper."

"Yes, but if you're going to meet with that book editor, you should consider buying a new outfit."

Rhiann bit her lower lip and nodded. "You might be right. Tell you what – if I get back to town in time, how about I swing by and pick you up and we could go together to Scottsdale?"

Her noticed her grandmother's sea-green eyes, so much like her sister's, light up. "I think I'd like that. I enjoy Old Town! And I'd love to help you find a special outfit."

Rhiann smiled and then asked, "Ready to tackle the crowd?"

"Maybe late on a Sunday afternoon, it won't be so bad."

Rhiann frowned. "Grams, this is Mesa, Arizona in January. You know better."

Her grandmother shrugged. "An old lady can hope."

Chapter 5

That evening, Rhiann sat at the dining table, laptop propped in front of her. Two nearby lamps provided light as she concentrated on her article proposal. The landline inside the villa rang; Rhiann answered.

"Hello?"

"Is this Rhiann?" a male voice asked.

"Who's calling please?" she responded without directly answering the question.

"Elias Griffin."

She smiled at the recognition. "Oh, hi, Elias. Yes, this is Rhiann. Sorry for the suspicion – I'm not used to having this phone ring late in the evening or hearing a man's voice on the other end."

"No problem. I've warned my mother to be cautious. Lots of scammers out there."

"Yeah. We only give this number to a few people."

"Your grandmother gave it to my mother. I think they plan a few activities together."

"So I heard."

"Listen, I've spent a few hours with mom this evening and was about to head home. I wondered if you'd join me for a drink at the bar before I leave."

"Umm, well, I..." She stumbled over what to say. "I'm finishing up a magazine story proposal, and it is getting a bit late."

"It's only nine. Don't tell me you're on the same night schedule as my mom and your grandmother."

"I am more of a morning person, but I often take advantage of Grams' going to be bed early to get some writing done," she retorted.

"Sorry. I came across crankier than I meant to," he said in a softer tone. "Sometimes the driving between Tucson and Mesa gets to me. In fact, I'm thinking of selling the Tucson gallery this year. One of my New Year's resolutions was to explore that option. Perhaps another time then for a drink."

"Elias, wait! No, that's fine. I apologize for my tartness." She sighed. "I'm, uh, I'm in the middle of a couple of things and sometimes my mouth blurts before my mind thinks. I'm not as good of juggling several things at once as I used to be."

He chuckled. "I know what you mean. Another reason I'm considering selling the Tucson business."

"Give me fifteen minutes. I need to finish a few thoughts for my article proposal, and I'll meet you at the bar."

"You sure? I don't want to interrupt if you're on a writing streak."

"I can complete it in the morning. I just have to finish two thoughts while they're still in my head."

"Okay then, great! Since the night sky is so pretty, I'll get us a table outside. What do you want me to order for you?"

"That's okay – I'll get something when I'm there. See you soon."

"Looking forward to it."

She heard him click off and then she hung up the phone. Rhiann walked back to her computer and typed out another half a dozen sentences, saved her document, and shut the laptop down.

Rhiann walked down the short hall to her grandmother's room. A small light was still on. She tapped on the door and entered when Grams said, "Come in."

She walked into the dimly lit room. Grams held a book as she leaned upon the pillows propped against the headboard of the bed.

"I just wanted you to know I'm meeting Elias for a drink at the bar," Rhiann explained. "I'll be back in an hour or less."

Grams smiled. "That's nice, dear. He seems like a good man."

"It's not a date, Grams."

"Rhiann ..."

The younger woman held a hand up. "No, Grams, I've made my decision. No more dating, no matter where we're living. I'm focusing on what life has for us, for me with writing and pet rescue and helping you find a place in Montana and getting us settled. I can't let complications, like dating and relationships, distract me."

"But honey, you might be missing out ..."

"Grams, you want us to move to Montana. I can't have a relationship with a guy in Arizona."

Grams removed her glasses from her nose and rubbed her fingers below her eyes.

"I guess that makes sense. Rhiann, I'm so sorry I've disrupted your life. This hasn't been fair to you."

Rhiann walked over and sat on the side of her grandmother's bed. She took the older woman's hand.

"Please don't think or say things like that. It's my honor to take care of you. I am fine. Brandon was the love of my life, and when he made the choice to put career above our relationship, well, you know that hurt me deeply. I don't trust men anyway, so becoming involved with someone isn't meant to be for me. I'm very willing to be friends with Elias, but I won't let my heart rule my head again. I have too much good in my life to ruin it taking a risk on some man, especially a man I wouldn't be seeing except in winter months." Silence passed between them for a few moments. "Now, you get ready to go to sleep. I have my cell phone if you need me. Otherwise, I'll see you in the morning."

She kissed her grandmother's cheek and rose from the woman's bedside.

"Well, once we get to Montana, you may change your mind about men. Just wait and see. I have a feeling a Montana man is going to sweep you off your feet!"

Rhiann chuckled. "Good night, Grams."

"Good night, my darling granddaughter. I love you."

"I love you, too, Grams, more than you'll ever know."

Rhiann closed the door and leaned against it for a moment. A flashback hit her like a freight train.

"You can't be serious?" Brandon said.

"My grandparents need me. I told you that."

"And I told you I'm not moving to Washington."

"Then, I guess I go without you."

"I guess you do. The ring, please. I'll be returning it."

He held out his hand, and with tears streaming down her face, Rhiann removed the diamond engagement ring and placed it into his outstretched hand.

As she shook the memory from her brain, Rhiann sighed and murmured, "No one will sweep me off my feet again."

Chapter 6

Holiday lights sparkled like diamonds inside the bar as Rhiann stood at the counter and ordered a glass of Chardonnay. As she awaited the drink, she glanced around, taking in the still-festive scene. In addition to the white garland of lights around the bar's counter, additional crystalline rope lights encircled wooden posts scattered throughout the building, and large, round red and green ornaments suspended from the ceiling.

She noticed no sign of Elias, and then she recalled him saying he planned to sit outdoors to enjoy the night sky. She glanced out onto the patio. Her eyes captured two older couples sitting as a small group and a pair of older women seated across from one another. No Elias.

The bartender brought her glass of wine.

"Eight dollars, please, ma'am," the thirty-something man said with a smile.

After paying him, Rhiann strolled through the aisle which led to the bistro-style outdoor setting. After a few glances around the patio, she spotted Elias toward the back of the gathering area and walked toward him. He looked up from pursuing his cell phone, saw her, and stood. He smiled and pulled out a chair for her.

"Good to see you, Rhiann," he said.

"Thank you," she responded in a quiet tone.

She set her wine glass on the table and sat down. Elias slid the chair closer to the small, metal table, and she thanked him again.

"My pleasure. I'm glad you could join me."

"Did you and your mom golf again this afternoon?" she asked.

Elias shook his head. "I took her grocery shopping and then we spent a few hours at the botanical gardens. She really enjoys those kinds of places. She grows several types of flowers at her home in Missoula, and she's interested in learning more about desert flora while she's here."

"Has she been to the Arizona Sonora Desert Museum in Tucson?"

Again, Elias shook his head. "Not yet, but it's on our to-do list."

Rhiann smiled. "Well, if you don't mind Grams and I taking her, we plan to be in Tucson on Friday; we thought we'd invite her. We also talked about visiting your gallery while we're in town."

He smiled. "That would be great! I think she'd like to go with you. I appreciate you thinking of her."

The smile remained on Rhiann's face. "Grams enjoys making new friends, and she loves the desert museum."

"It is a wonderful place." He took a sip of his drink. "How's the rest of your day been?" he asked afterward.

"Good. I took Grams to the grocery store, too, and while she played bridge this afternoon, I took the time to work on my article and on a proposal I plan to send for the story I talked with you and your mother about."

He smiled. "Busy lady."

She shrugged. "That's one thing I like about freelancing – I can do it anywhere, at least anywhere that I have internet access. Grams has come to Arizona for the winters for several years, and because I can take my work wherever, it all works out." She sipped her wine.

"I'm glad your mom agreed to be interviewed for the story I'm proposing to the magazine."

"It's a cool idea, and I know she's thrilled you asked."

"I hope to find a few more people at the resort who are from Montana."

"Beneficial not only for your story, but also for your grandmother since she wants to move there. Why leave Spokane, though? Especially at her age."

Rhiann shrugged and, after taking another sip of wine, she said, "She was born and raised there, leaving after nursing school to serve at a veteran's hospital in Boise. Since Grandpops died about eight years ago, Grams has been talking about returning to Montana. With her heart condition, though, I've been able to persuade her the trips to Arizona are enough, and to uproot herself totally wouldn't be the best idea. During the past year, however, she's become more adamant. She knows I want to start an animal sanctuary, and she's totally convinced Montana is the place to do that."

"An animal sanctuary? Wow, that's a big undertaking. What type of sanctuary?"

"Have you been to Best Friends in southern Utah?"

Elias shook his head and then took another drink from his old-fashioned glass. Rhiann guessed it to be whiskey as the fragrance wafted her way.

"It's a rescue facility for all types of animals," Rhiann continued, "from dogs and cats to birds and livestock. The organization has been around for more than thirty years, rescuing and caring for animals in need and adopting as many as they can. Do you remember the Michael Vick dogfighting scandal?"

"Oh, yes. That was all over the news!"

Rhiann nodded. "Best Friends is one of the facilities where some of the dogs were placed. The staff worked with the dogs, and several were able to be rehabilitated and adopted. Others lived out their lives at the sanctuary."

"You want to take in dogs from fighting rings?"

She shook her head. "I'll leave that up to the experts, like Best Friends. I want to provide a sanctuary for animals in need of a home, whether they've been abandoned, neglected, or the owner can't care for them any longer. Even puppy mill dogs, which is a major issue, mostly in the Midwest, but they can pop up anywhere."

"What's a puppy mill dog?"

"One that's raised specifically to make money for the owner. There are reputable breeders and there are unscrupulous breeders, the kind that keep numerous dogs, often small breeds, in kennels with little social interaction, oftentimes poor food and little to no medical care. These people are also known as backyard breeders. Their only goal is to make money from puppies, so they breed the females as often as possible. They sells the pups either to pet stores, which thankfully are becoming less known for special breed dogs and more helpful toward rescue and shelter dogs, or they sell online or in newspapers."

Elias sat back in his chair. "Wow! I never realized that was happening."

"A lot of people don't. There's a great need for education, which is something else I try to do."

"I appreciate you educating me." He took a deep breath, glanced around the area, and then returned his eyes to Rhiann. "I've been thinking about getting a dog for Mother to help keep her company since dad died a few years ago. She's resisted the idea as being too much for her, but she's young enough yet to care for a pet. We had a few cats while I was growing up, but they were mostly outdoor animals to keep the mice population down. Mom enjoyed them, though, I remember that."

"My grandmother has a cat that's been great company for her. Her name is Poppy, and she travels with us on these winter vacations. Animals are great companions, especially for seniors – helps keep them active and engaged with life. What kind of dog are you looking for?"

He shrugged.

"Not sure. She wants to spend some time here first and maybe, if she decides to get one, do it before she returns home in the spring. Or even wait until she gets back to Missoula."

Rhiann nodded. "That may be best since she'll be here only a few more months."

Silence again enveloped them as they each enjoyed their drinks for a few moments.

"How's your wine?" Elias asked.

"Wonderful! Chardonnay is one of my favorites, especially on warm nights like this."

He smiled. "I'll remember that."

She looked at him and took a deep breath. Then she said, "Um, Elias, I need to be forthright with you. I don't date."

Surprise reflected in his silver-black eyes.

Rhiann entwined her fingers as she looked at him and continued, "I think you're fascinating, and I'm delighted to get to know you better, but I'm not looking for a relationship, a boyfriend, or any type of romantic tie. I've been burned in the past, badly burned, in fact, and the last few dates I did go on were horrible. I'm not going down that road again. I'm focusing on my writing career and caring for my grandmother, and hopefully, starting an animal sanctuary."

"I'm sorry to hear that," he responded in a quiet voice. "I mean, not about the sanctuary, but about not dating. I had hoped to ask you out."

"I wondered, so I wanted to be honest with you from the outset." She stood, holding her half-filled wine glass. "I'll take my leave then."

Elias grabbed her hand, and she looked at him.

"No. Please, stay," he said. "I, uh, I respect your honesty, and I now know where you're coming from." He removed his hand from hers. "Please, sit, finish your drink."

"Are you sure?" Rhiann asked.

He nodded and smiled. "Yes. I'm enjoying our conversation, and I'd like to get to know you better. A new friend is always good to find."

She smiled. "I'm glad you feel that way. I do, too."

Rhiann returned to her seat, picked up her wine glass, and held it toward him. "To making new friends."

He grinned and chimed his glass with hers. They each sipped their drinks.

"You said on the phone you're thinking of selling your Tucson gallery?" Rhiann asked Elias.

He nodded, and she gave him a brief smile. "I guess it's a good thing Grams and I are planning to visit next week," Rhiann said. "Is it because of the commute?"

"Partly, yes, but it's also becoming more difficult to manage two locations," he responded. "I had three up until five years ago. I sold the Sedona gallery, which is the first one I started. Way too much travel."

"What made you move farther south? I've been to Sedona a few times – it's spectacular!"

Elias smiled. "That it is, but it's also become incredibly expensive and an extremely competitive market. Lots of artists, lots of galleries. And it doesn't draw the snowbirds or the spring training baseball teams like Phoenix and Tucson do."

Rhiann nodded. "I can see that. More year-round traffic here, I imagine."

"Summers not so much because they can be brutally hot, as you likely know, but with hundreds of thousands of residents, the galleries are always busy. We do a lot of festivals and other events during the fall, winter, and spring, so that helps to tide us through the slower summer months. I love bringing in various artists, and I do so every few weeks. But managing staff in both locations is wearing on me as is the commute, as you say. And if mom decides she wants to continue snowbirding down here, I want to have more time with her."

Again, Rhiann nodded. "Time with family is precious, that's for sure."

She sipped from her wine glass again, and Elias drained his drink.

"Can I order you another?" he asked. "I'm getting one more for me."

She smiled. "No thanks. I have a dog transport tomorrow, so I'd better hold to one so I can wake up early in the morning."

"What's a dog transport?"

Rhiann smiled. "You're not much into the pet thing, are you?"

He shook his head. "No, not really. I don't mind animals – in fact, I keep a dish of water and a bench outside the galleries because

I've noticed a large increase in the number of people strolling the streets with their dogs."

"Well, thank you for doing that," Rhiann said.

"It's kind of for selfish reasons. Sometimes it draws people into the galleries. One will sit on the bench with the dog while the other comes into the building to look. Sometimes they'll come back later and make a purchase."

He smiled, and she returned it.

"Not a bad business move," Rhiann said.

"So, what is a dog transport?"

"I help rescue groups get animals from one place to another. Sometimes the animal is going into rescue from another organization, and sometimes I'm helping get the dog or cat to its new adoptive family. We're like a long chain, and each transporter is a link in that chain. Animals can travel hundreds of miles thanks to volunteer transporters. I once took a dog that started in Seattle and ended up in Minneapolis, from rescue to its new home. I was just one link in that transport chain."

"Amazing!"

Rhiann smiled. "Tomorrow I'm heading to Flagstaff and bringing a couple of dogs down from the city animal shelter. They'll be going into rescue down here. And then in a few days, I drive to the New Mexico border to pick up three dogs. Two of them will be fostered in Tucson."

He raised his eyebrows. "You'll be in Tucson later this week?"

She nodded. "Just for a short time, taking the two dogs to their foster home. The other is being fostered in Maricopa, so I'll be bringing it back this way."

"What's a foster home?"

Rhiann chuckled. "I do get to educate you on pet rescue. That's okay – I was in your shoes a few years back."

"Let me grab another drink and we can continue this conversation." He stood and then looked at her. "Are you sure I can't get you another Chardonnay?"

"I'm sure. But a glass of ice water would be nice."

He smiled. "Ice water it is. I'll be right back."

Elias walked away, heading into the bar. Rhiann pulled out her phone and noticed a text message. "Transport for tomorrow confirmed. Check your email for the details."

Her fingers jumped to the email icon, and she skimmed until she saw the message. She read the information and quickly typed a note into her phone. She finished just as Elias returned to the table.

"Everything okay?" he asked.

She nodded. "Just confirming my transport for tomorrow. All is well."

He smiled and sat down. "Good to hear. So, to continue my pet rescue education – what's a foster home?"

Chapter 7

The next afternoon, driving south of Flagstaff toward Phoenix, Rhiann glanced in the back seat at the two dog crates. An amber and white Shih tzu lay in one and a white Maltese lay in the other. Rhiann smiled. "You two are likely going to spoiled and doted on, both at the rescue and when you get new homes," she said aloud. "How cute you are!"

As she neared the town of Peoria, a northern suburb of Phoenix, she decided she had enough time to make a slight detour. "I think Grams would like to meet you two," she murmured.

Taking a round-about way so as not to hit Phoenix proper, she exited the interstate and headed toward Peoria. She pulled off into a strip mall and reset her car's GPS for the resort. Then she made a quick phone call.

"Jennifer, it's Rhiann. I want my Grams to see the dogs before I bring them to you. Can I meet you at your house this evening and drop them off? Then Grams and I can eat dinner out before heading back to Cave Creek."

Rhiann waited a response and smiled. "Thank you! I appreciate this. I'll call you when we leave. Give me your address again if you don't mind. It's been awhile since I brought dogs to your house instead of to the adoption center."

She wrote down the address her fellow rescue worker provided. "Great! I'll call you in about two hours."

After clicking off her cell phone, Rhiann glanced at the small dogs once again. "Grams is going to be surprised to see you!"

After making sure no traffic was close, she maneuvered her RAV back onto the street and followed the GPS to the resort. Rhiann garnered her usual parking spot and brought the SUV to a stop. She left her wallet in the glovebox, and after exiting her vehicle, she opened the back door and pulled out both crates. One in each hand, she carried them to her grandmother's villa.

She set the kennel containing the Shih tzu onto the pavement and unlocked the adobe structure's front door. Her foot braced the heavy wooden door as she retrieved the dog crates, and then she carried them inside.

She found her grandmother and Elias' mother seated in the living room. Rhiann smiled.

"Hi, ladies. Nice to see you both."

Rhiann walked closer to the women, each sitting in a chair with a small table and lamp between them.

"Look what I brought," Rhiann said with a smile.

She set the two crates on the floor.

"Oh, puppies!" Grams exclaimed.

"Not quite," Rhiann responded, smile still on her face.

She drew out the Maltese first. Grams' eyes lit up and she held out her arms. Rhiann placed the little dog into Grams' embrace. The older woman hugged the cuddly, soft-coated dog against her chest and cooed, "Oh, how precious!"

"It's adorable!" Helen said, watching Martha.

A smile still on her face, Rhiann took the Shih tzu with its travel crate and held up the little animal. She saw Helen's face light up.

"What a beautiful dog!"

"Would you like to hold her?" Rhiann asked.

"Oh, may I?"

Rhiann nodded and placed the quivering dog on Helen's lap. Immediately, the older woman began stroking the dog's fur.

"They both came from the Flagstaff shelter," Rhiann explained. "Their special person passed away, and no one in the family wanted them. They're both older. Maggie, the Maltese, is eleven, and Star, the shih tzu, is ten. Older dogs, even if they're small breeds, aren't adopted easily from shelters, so the rescue in Phoenix that I work with had them released to them. I'm taking them into the city for a better chance at being adopted, especially now that snowbirds have come in. Some couple may adopt them."

"Can they be separated?" Helen asked.

"They probably can be, but it may not be best for them. They likely need each other."

"Why is this one shaking so?" Helen asked.

"It's pretty traumatic going from a quiet home to a noisy shelter," Rhiann said.

"You came out of your way just to let us hug on them, to comfort them," Grams said.

"I did indeed! I'm glad Helen is here, too, so she can see what rescue is about," Rhiann said, reaching over to stroke the Shih tzu's head. "Besides, they've been in the car long enough – I thought they needed a break."

Grams gave the Maltese a loving hug and then said, "I bet they need a potty break. Why don't you take them out back? We can all sit on the patio for a few minutes."

"Sounds good, Grams," Rhiann said, taking the Maltese from her.

She turned toward Helen, who said, as she hugged the Shih tzu closer, "I'll carry this one."

As she and Helen walked to the patio door leading to the back yard, Rhiann had a feeling the Shih tzu may have found a new home. *But what about the Maltese?*

FOUR HOURS LATER, THE three women walked into Elias' downtown Phoenix art gallery.

"I'm so excited for the two of you to see my son's gallery – it's quite incredible!" Helen said, a lilt in her voice.

"You're very proud of him, aren't you?" Grams said to her new friend.

"Oh, most certainly!" replied Helen, a large smile on his face. "He's found great success here in Arizona. "His father was proud of him as well. Elias certainly found his calling here, between his own photography and opening the different galleries. I had hoped he would have kept the Sedona business, but I think managing three in different locations would have been too much."

Helen led the way into the ornate building. Glass windows floor to ceiling greeted the women, and once they stepped inside, oil and watercolor paintings, Native American baskets and pottery, bronze sculptures, and landscape photographs welcomed them. Rhiann and Grams gazed around in awe. In less than a minute, Rhiann heard Elias' rich, deep voice.

"Ladies! Welcome! I'm so pleased to see you. So, Mother, did you put in an adoption application for the dog?"

Rhiann turned to face him and saw a genuine smile upon his face. Her heart fluttered a bit as he gazed into her eyes. *Cool it, Rhiann*, her brain chastised. *You cannot fall for this guy.*

"I sure did," Helen replied to her son's question. "I hope I'm approved."

Elias kissed his mother's cheek. "I don't know why you wouldn't be. You raised me and I'm not a bad guy."

He looked at Rhiann and his eyes twinkled. She blushed slightly and looked away, pretending to study an oil painting of a southwestern sunrise landscape.

A moment later, she felt Grams pinch her forearm. When she looked at her grandmother and saw the motion of her head, she followed the two older women as Elias led them farther into the gallery. She glanced around. Paintings hung on the wall, and pottery and sculptures set on white pillars throughout the large room. Landscape photographs of desert scenes, mountain vistas, and various wildlife species also adorned the gallery. Rhiann wondered if any of the framed photos were taken by Elias.

"This is my favorite photograph Elias has taken," Helen said, answering Rhiann's silent question.

The woman pointed to a snow-capped mountain scene in autumn. Tree leaves of crimson and gold scattered throughout the photograph beneath the mountain setting. A large, lightly ice-covered pond highlighted the left side of the photograph, and a bull moose stood in the middle of the waterway.

"That's fantastic," Grams said, looking closely at the photograph.

"It is striking," Rhiann agreed. "Where did you take this, Elias?"

He grinned. "About thirty miles from Mother's house."

Grams smiled. "I thought it was a Montana scene. My family and I used to see big guys like this near our homestead." She sighed. "The beauty of that state is unforgettable."

Grams turned and looked at Rhiann. "Did you see things like this when you lived near West Yellowstone that year?"

"Nothing quite like this guy, no. But yes, I saw moose quite often," Rhiann replied. "And bison."

"You lived near the western gate to Yellowstone National Park?" Elias asked, looking at Rhiann.

She nodded. "I freelanced stories about the area for more than a year."

Grams smiled, and with a sense of pride, said, "A story that she wrote from that time is being published by *Big Sky Magazine*. It's about a moose in fact."

"Really?" Helen said. "How wonderful!"

"Is that the article you were working on when we first met?" Elias asked, again looking at Rhiann.

She smiled. "That's the one."

"I'd like to hear more about it," he responded. "Let's finish our tour and then I'll take you ladies to dinner."

As her son began to walk toward an alcove, Helen leaned toward Grams and whispered, "Our children are creative, something else they have in common."

Rhiann heard Helen's comment and looked at the woman. She discovered Helen and Grams looking at her, small smiles on their faces.

Chapter 8

The next morning, Rhiann and Grams sat on the patio chairs in the backyard of their shared cottage. Two coffee cups lined the table in front of them. Grams read the screen of her tablet, and Poppy lay stretched out on the grass while Rhiann finished a conversation with her rescue friend, Jennifer, from Scottsdale.

"I thought so, too, so yes, I agree." She paused. "Oh, really? Well, that might work. I'll talk with Mrs. Griffin today and get back with you. Thanks, Jenn."

She hung up and looked at her grandmother who glanced up from her tablet. "Was that about the Shih tzu?"

Rhiann nodded. "Jenn doesn't want to separate the dogs, which I suspected. But she has another possibility."

"That's good news." Grams drank a bit from her coffee cup and then continues, "The dogs you're transporting in a couple of days – are those another group from the reservation in New Mexico?"

Rhiann nodded. "I'll be bringing three dogs back. Two I'll leave off with a foster in Tucson; the other dog will be fostered in Maricopa."

"When do you meet with that book editor?"

"Next week. Another trip to Tucson."

"Didn't Elias say one of his galleries is located in Tucson?"

"Yes, he did."

"Maybe I'll go with you. I'd enjoy seeing his gallery, especially if it's anything like the one in Phoenix. Would that be all right with you, dear?"

Rhiann smiled. "Of course, Grams. We could have lunch after my meeting and then go to the gallery. Maybe Mrs. Griffin would like to join us. I believe they said she hasn't yet been to his Tucson building."

"That's a wonderful idea! But what can we do while you're at your meeting?"

"I'll drop the two of you off at the desert museum. We can eat lunch there and then stop by Elias' gallery."

Her grandmother smiled. "I'm liking this idea more and more. We didn't get to go to the desert museum last winter."

Rhiann returned her grandmother's smile. "I really enjoy that place, and I think it would be fun to take Elias' mother and let her experience it as well."

Grams patted Rhiann's arm. "Thank you, dear. Thank you for letting two old ladies tag along. I know this meeting is extremely important. In case I haven't said it lately, I'm immensely proud of you. Your parents would be, too, I know that."

Tears glistened in Rhiann's eyes. "I'd like to think that."

Her grandmother squeezed her arm. "Believe me, I know they would be. When are you going to tell Erin about the book?"

"When I know it's a done deal. I don't want to put the cart before the horse."

Grams smiled. "Let's get something special for dinner that night; maybe pick up something in Tucson," she said. "I have a strong feeling we'll be celebrating that evening."

Rhiann leaned over and kissed her grandmother's cheek. "You always have the most optimistic outlook on things, Grams."

The older woman looked at her granddaughter. "Why think negatively or be pessimistic about something that hasn't happened yet? You know my philosophy follows that of Norman Vincent Peale – 'the power of positive thinking.'"

"That's one reason you're a strong woman, Grams."

"So are you, my dear. So are you."

Rhiann smiled. "Well, I haven't always felt that way."

"Growing older, experiencing more of the ups and downs of life, teaches us wisdom and gives us strength. You've grown a lot in the past twenty years, sweetheart."

"Sometimes I wish I would have been wiser and stronger back then," Rhiann replied. She stood, stretched slightly, and added, "I'll go see Mrs. Griffin and let her know what Jennifer told me. I'll be back in a few minutes."

She walked inside the villa, through the living room, and unlocked the front door. As she stepped outside, she nearly collided with Elias.

"Oh!" Rhiann said, taking a step backward.

She looked up at his smiling face.

"Sorry. I didn't mean to startle you. I was just stopping by to talk with you about the dog my mother is interested in," he said.

"And I was planning to go see her in a few minutes about the same," Rhiann said with a slight smile. She took a step away from the door. "Take a short walk with me?"

"Of course," Elias replied, and they began walking side-by-side toward the pool.

"I called Jennifer, my rescue contact in the city, and spoke with her about your mother's interest in the Shih tzu. She agreed with me that the dogs shouldn't be separated. They've been together for about eight years, according to the family, and since all of this is traumatic for them – the death of their person, going into a shelter, coming down here – it's best they be adopted together. Jennifer has two couples interested in them already."

"Mom's going to be disappointed," Elias commented, a touch of sadness in his voice. "That picture you showed me last night ... I think that dog would have been perfect for my mom."

Rhiann smiled. "I know your mother was taken with it. The good news is Jennifer has another Shih tzu. It's been on a medical hold for the past few months as the dog needed to be spayed, vaccinated, and groomed plus some dental work – she wasn't taken care of very well – and she needed a bit more socialization. She'll be available in another day, so I thought I'd take your mother to meet this dog if she would be interested. Jennifer sent me a picture."

Rhiann pulled out her phone, turned it on, and pressed her message key. She held up a photo of a brown and white Shih tzu, freshly clipped, which Jennifer had sent. Rhiann watched a smile come upon Elias' face.

"That's a cute one!"

"Do you think your mom would want to meet her?"

His eyes met hers. "Yes, I'm sure of it. Let's go talk with her."

They wandered to Helen's cottage two rows over from Grams'.

"I'm glad you and your grandmother are close to my mother's place," Elias said. "She's been overjoyed to become your grandmother's friend and to become more active in the community here. The two of you have a lot to do with her happiness here."

"I know Grams enjoys your mother's company," Rhiann replied. "The two are good for each other. In fact, Grams and I were talking this morning – I have a meeting in Tucson later this week, and Grams wants to go to the desert museum. We thought we'd ask your mother if she wants to go."

She stopped and looked at Elias. "Do you think she would?"

His eyes softened as he looked at her. Smiling, he responded, "I think she'd greatly enjoy that. You could all come to my gallery while you're in town as well."

Rhiann smiled. "I know we'd like that."

As she began to walk toward Helen's home again, Elias gently took her hands into his. Rhiann paused and looked into his eyes.

"I want to thank you and your grandmother for befriending my mom. Like I said, the two of you have a lot to do with her happiness here, and that means a lot to me. Your friendship has been good for me, too, and I want to thank you for that as well."

For a moment, she thought he'd try to kiss her. Instead, as he looked into her eyes, he asked, "In fact, if you don't mind me asking a favor ...."

"What is it?" Rhiann responded in a halting voice.

"I was wondering, since you'll be in Tucson in a few days, if you could stop by the gallery to pick up some of my framed photographs and bring them back to my Phoenix establishment? It would help me out a lot and save me making the trip back and forth twice in the day."

"Don't you have to come back anyway?"

Elias shook his head. "I keep a condo in Tucson where I stay when I'm at that gallery two or more days in a row, which happens frequently. I have more trustworthy employees in Phoenix than I do in Tucson. Another reason to sell that gallery. I wouldn't have to deal with those less trustworthy employees."

"A lot goes into making and maintaining a business, doesn't it?"

He gave her a brief smile and released her hands. Rhiann experienced the feeling of warmth flutter away.

"You'll learn more about that as you start your animal sanctuary," he said. "A person can't do it all by himself ... or herself. You need a team, a crew, and they need to be trustworthy or they'll steal you blind."

"Sounds like you're talking from experience," Rhiann said.

He nodded. "Yep. Happened twice in the last few years. Happened several times in Sedona, too. That's another reason I sold the gallery there." He took a deep breath. "So, could you do it? Deliver the photographs to Phoenix?"

"If timing allows, sure; I'd be happy to."

He smiled. "Thanks, Rhiann. I'd appreciate your help."

They again began walking toward Elias' mother's villa.

"You need to know, though, Elias, transports don't always go according to plan. The dogs I'll be dealing with come from the reservation, and they are often somewhat feral and elusive. I can keep you posted on timing, as I'll be doing with the foster parents."

He nodded. "Time isn't a problem. Since I'll be staying at the condo, I can meet you whenever you get to town." He gave her a business card. "This is how you can reach me. Both the gallery number and my cell number are on the card."

She accepted the offering from his outstretched hand and nodded. "I'll keep you informed on how the transport is going and about the time I expect to get to Tucson."

He smiled and squeezed her hands. "Thank you, Rhiann. Now, shall we go see Mother about adopting a dog?"

She smiled back.

"Yes, yes, we shall."

Chapter 9

That evening, Rhiann, Grams, Elias, and his mother left the resort's restaurant.

"I can't believe I'm getting a dog!" Helen said, a touch of laughter in her voice.

"Well, believe it, Mom, for in another day you'll be a dog owner," Elias said, a smile on his face. "Thanks to Rhiann here."

He looked at her with twinkling eyes. Rhiann blushed slightly.

"I'm glad it all worked out," she replied.

"I'm happy for you, Helen," Grams said. "I know how much my Poppy cat means to me, and how the different animals on our orchard all those years ago brought so much joy. Rhiann's grandfather and I had hoped to be able to leave that property to her for her animal sanctuary that she's been wanting for so long. Alas, we couldn't do it."

Rhiann placed a tender hand upon her grandmother's arm. "No worries, Grams. It just wasn't meant to be."

"But now that you're thinking of moving to Montana, your rescue sanctuary can happen," Helen said.

"If we can find a property, and if we can even afford land there," Rhiann stated with a firmness in her voice. "Nothing is certain yet."

"I'm the more optimistic one in the family," Grams said. "I'm sure we'll find something wonderful. Montana is a large, beautiful state.

Helen nodded, a smile on her face. "That it is."

"There's plenty of time to look for locations," Elias interjected. "It's not even February. There are lots of weeks and months to iron out the future."

"You are right, Elias," Grams agreed. "Sometimes I just get so excited thinking about returning to my home state, I feel like a whirlwind, wanting to get things decided quickly."

He stopped walking and turned to Rhiann with a smile. "I just want to thank Rhiann here for helping my mother adopt a furry friend. Whether she's living down here in the winter or up north in the summer, she'll have this wonderful dog to keep her company, to go on walks with, and to help her garden."

Rhiann chuckled. "Yep, maybe even doing the digging for her!"

Everyone laughed and continued walking. They stopped at Helen's apartment first, leaving her off at the door. Elias kissed his mother's cheek.

"I'll stop back over before I leave," he said. "I want to see Rhiann and Martha home."

"There's no need for that Elias," Rhiann said. "Grams and I are fine ..."

"A gentleman never lets a lady walk home alone, let alone her grandmother," he said.

"Good boy, Elias. I knew your dad and I raised you well," Helen said.

Turning to look at Rhiann and her grandmother, Helen continued, "Thank you both. I so appreciate your friendship! And Rhiann – thank you, thank you, for introducing me to Jennifer and that wonderful dog! I can't wait to bring Holly home! And such an appropriate name for my belated Christmas present."

Elias unlocked the door for his mother. "I'll be back in a few moments."

"All right, son. Good night, ladies," Helen said, acknowledging Rhiann and her grandmother.

"Good night, Helen," Grams said.

"Good night, Mrs. Griffin," Rhiann responded.

As she and Grams began walking to their own cottage, Elias fell in step beside Rhiann.

"I'm happy for your mother," Grams said to Elias. "Having a four-legged companion is such a delight!"

"I know you have your cat, but why not a dog? Especially with Rhiann's rescue endeavors."

Grams laughed. "Oh, we'd have plenty of dogs, more cats, too, if we could. We had two dogs at the farm that moved to town with us. But with my husband's illness and ultimate passing, as we lost each dog, we just didn't get another. Rhiann's had her hands full taking care of us. Miss Poppy found us four winters ago, and after our second dog died, well, it just seemed best to keep her an only child, so to speak. One day we'll get another dog, of that I'm sure."

"I get my dog fix each time I travel for rescue," Rhiann said with a smile. "It is easier with just Poppy for now, especially going back and forth every four to six months as we do."

They came to Grams' cottage. The older woman unlocked the door, and, glancing at her granddaughter and Elias, she said, "I'm glad your mother wants to go to Tucson with us and see the desert museum."

He smiled. "I appreciate you and Rhiann inviting her." He looked at Rhiann and his smile broadened. "A book deal! Wow, that's so incredible! I can't believe you left that part out of our conversation about your 'meeting' on Friday."

His smile and tone were playful.

"It's not for sure yet, Elias, remember? But, yes, I admit, I'm excited," Rhiann said with a grin.

"Too bad you have to make two trips to the Tucson area so close together," he said. "If you could combine your dog transport with meeting your editor ..."

Rhiann shook her head. "I have to plan a full day for the transport – a person just never knows what will come up. Besides, you want your mother to see the desert museum and the art gallery, don't you?"

She glanced at him and found him looking at her. "I want to see my mother, yes, and you, too." He looked at Grams. "And Martha, you as well."

The older woman smiled. "I appreciate that, Elias." She looked at Rhiann and then leaned over and kissed her granddaughter's cheek. "I'm quite proud of this one." She looked at Elias and said, "Thank you for the walk, Elias. I'll bid you goodnight."

She turned to Rhiann and said in a low voice, "Take your time."

As her grandmother went inside, Rhiann bit her lip to stifle a giggle.

"I like your grandmother," Elias said.

Rhiann looked at him, a smile on her face. "She's a likable lady."

"So are you," he said in a sultry voice.

"Elias," she started, a warning in her voice.

He cleared his throat. "Sorry. I do mean it, though. I like you, Rhiann."

She smiled and put a hand on his cheek. "And I like you. I'm just ... I'm not ready to travel the romance road at this time."

He nodded. He removed her hand and kissed the palm. "Sorry for stepping out of bounds."

As he dropped her hand, she smiled again. "I'll keep you informed on how the transport is going when I reach New Mexico and give you an approximate time I expect to get to Tucson with the dogs."

"That would be great. My thanks again, Rhiann – for everything." He kissed her cheek. "Good night and sleep well."

Elias took a step back.

Rhiann smiled. "You, too. Elias."

She watched him as he began walking toward his mother's cottage. She leaned against the doorframe of her grandmother's villa a moment and sighed.

I could so easily fall for this guy, she thought.

She sighed again and then went inside.

Chapter 10

The next day, Rhiann and Grams sat at a table on Helen's patio. The woman's newly adopted dog, Holly, explored the area. Helen brought out a shrimp cocktail appetizer and sat between them.

"This looks wonderful," Grams said to Helen.

"Elias is on his way – he was delayed at the Tucson gallery, but he should be here in about fifteen minutes," Helen said. "Oh, I can't wait for him to meet Holly!"

"She seems to be settling in well," Rhiann said. "She's enjoying exploring the yard."

Helen laid a hand on top of one of Rhiann's. "Thank you so much for helping me adopt her and for taking me shopping yesterday to buy what she needs. I'm indebted to you, Rhiann."

The younger woman shook her head. "No, you're not. It's a joy for me to help animals find new homes, and I know you and Holly are going to be happy together."

Helen patted Rhiann's hand and then looked at Grams. "Martha, you have such a lovely granddaughter."

Grams smiled. "She's a special girl all right."

"Oh, stop it, both of you!" Rhiann said with a smile.

The three ladies sipped tea from the glasses on the table and again observed Holly. The dog sniffed along the black-railed fence, seeming to absorb each scent she found.

"Remind me her story again," Grams commented.

"She was a breeding dog," Rhiann said. "For nearly seven years, she produced pups and now that's she's nearly nine, the breeder decided she was getting too old. I think Jennifer said only three of six in her last litter survived. Thankfully, the owner reached out to Jennifer's rescue and adoption center, and I believe the woman got an earful and some education from Jennifer about proper dog care and irresponsible breeding. That can be a problem and sometimes leads to cruelty, which, in Holly's case, was close to being so with the little vet care she received the past few years."

"Well, she has no worries about that anymore," Helen said in a firm tone.

A knock sounded on the front door, and as the women turned, a key twisted in the lock, and Elias stepped into the living room. Helen rose and walked to greet him.

"I'm glad you're here, son. Come meet my new dog!"

Rhiann glanced at her grandmother smiled.

"I think Helen is smitten with Holly," she whispered.

Grams patted Rhiann's hand. "Oh, no doubt. And I'd add, I think her son is smitten with you."

Rhiann glanced across the table and into the kitchen. Seeing the smile Elias gave her, she felt a blush crawl up her neck.

Grams whispered, "Might I say I think the feeling is mutual?"

"Shh! You know it can't be."

"Yes, it could. Stop hiding, sweetheart. Let the holiday spirit take you on a grand adventure with love."

Rhiann bit her lower lip. She turned her head to watch Holly continue investigating her new home.

"Be like Holly," Grams added in a low tone. "Like any of those dogs you rescue – they need courage and they need to learn to trust."

Rhiann looked at her grandmother and then at Elias when he stepped closer to the table. He smiled at her and then glanced at the dog.

"So, you played matchmaker," he said.

Startled, Rhiann asked, "What?"

He looked at her. "My mother and the dog – you brought them together."

Rhiann blushed as her grandmother chuckled.

LATER THAT EVENING, Rhiann and Elias strolled along the pathway between Helen's cottage and the pool area. Christmas lights still adorned the nearby saguaro cacti and other plants as well as the pool area, bar, and restaurant.

"One reason I love coming to Arizona in January is because the holiday lights stay up the whole month," Rhiann told Elias. "I know that's a reason Grams likes coming here in January, too."

"Nothing like a saguaro decorated with lights," he said, a slight laugh to his voice.

"I like them," Rhiann reiterated.

"Me, too, but I do enjoy a tall fir tree now and then," he said.

"So do we – that's the type of tree we get each December," she said.

Elias smiled. "Another thing we have in common."

"What about your mother? Does she have a fir tree in her home at Christmas?"

Elias shook his head. "She puts up an artificial tree. She stopped using real trees after Dad died. Too much work for her alone."

"Grams might not have a live tree if I didn't bring one home."

He stopped walking, turned to her, smiled, and said, "Don't tell me you're Paul Bunyan and go out and chop one yourself?"

She returned his smile. "If I had a pickup tree to haul it in, I likely would. No, I use a local tree farm."

Rhiann looked around at the lights twinkling around the resort. "We get the best of both worlds coming south after the New Year – evergreens in December and saguaros in January."

"Have you and your grandmother decided how long you'll stay this year yet?"

Rhiann shook her head. "Depends on the weather up north. We usually stay until at least mid-April. I try to take Grams to some spring training games in March. With the book to work on though, providing I get a contract, we likely won't be able to see as many games this year."

"Which team is her favorite?"

"Well, Seattle Mariners, of course!"

She grinned, and he smiled back.

"Of course!"

Their eyes, filled with merriment, locked on each other. Rhiann stared at Elias' smokey gray eyes, drawn by the delight and desire she saw in them. Momentarily, she wondered what her emerald orbs conveyed.

Elias's left hand touched her face. "You're quite a woman, you know that? Freelance writer, dog rescuer, caregiver, book author, baseball enthusiast ..." Rhiann smiled. He stroked her cheek. "I'm very taken with you, Rhiann."

She bit her lower lip. His hand slid lower on her face, and a finger gently roved over her bottom lip. A jolt, like a bolt of electricity, shot through her.

"I know what you said about dating, about romantic involvement," Elias whispered, "but I really want to kiss you right now."

Rhiann's eyes remained locked upon his and a small smile came to her face.

"Nothing says friends can't share a kiss," she said, hearing a sensuous tone in her own voice.

I'm a goner, shot through her brain as she watched Elias' face inch closer to hers. Rhiann closed her eyes. Her heart pounded in anticipation, and when Elias' lips closed over hers, Rhiann savored the sweetness. They tasted one another tenderly, once then twice, exploring both the experience and one another's reactions. As their lips parted, Rhiann smiled. She felt Elias' forehead against hers. She kept her eyes closed, relishing the feelings she had locked away for years.

Elias stepped away and a wave of cold hit Rhiann immediately. She looked at him. He was studying her face.

"I hope you change your mind about just being friends," he said in a soft voice.

"Perhaps ... perhaps I can ... I can at least think about it," she whispered.

He took a step and closed the gap between them again. His hands encircled her forearms. He bent his head and brushed his lips against her cheek.

"Let me try to persuade you," he murmured.

His mouth captured hers with passion. Startled, yet also excited, Rhiann closed her eyes. As she allowed her lips to dance with his, she delighted in newly re-discovered emotions. She wrapped her arms around his neck. Elias deepened the kiss, taking her breath away and inciting and awakening feelings long buried.

Elias drew away and again lay his forehead against hers.

"I take it we mean more to each other than friends?"

She smiled. "Friendship is a good place to start ... but this is good, too."

His head bent down to entrap her lips again. However, Rhiann placed her hands on his chest and took a step backward.

"I think ... I think it's time to continue our walk," she said. Elias looked into her eyes. "I need to take things slowly, Elias. I haven't ... I haven't been kissed like that, or kissed back like that, in a long time."

A lazy smile dawned on his face. "Could have fooled me." He tucked her hand into his elbow. "Shall we saunter, my lady?"

She returned his smile and gave him a nod. "So we shall."

They walked a paved pathway near the restaurant, talking quietly and absorbing the halo of lights around the resort.

Chapter 11

The next morning, Rhiann lay in bed, pillows propped against her head and back. She picked up her cell phone to check the time for what seemed the twentieth time. She sighed, tossed her phone onto the bed, and snuggled back into the covers.

"I really need to get moving," she murmured.

A hesitant knock sounded on her bedroom door.

"Rhiann? Darling? Are you awake?"

Grams' voice noted a tone of concern.

"Yes, Grams, I'm awake. I'll be out in a few moments."

"Don't you have that transport today?"

"Yes." She sat up in bed again. "You can come in."

Her grandmother opened the door and peeked inside. "Are you okay?"

Rhiann sighed. "I honestly don't know."

Grams stepped into Rhiann's room, holding Poppy in her arms. "Our girl here was meowing by your door. I think she's worried about you."

Rhiann gave a slight smile. "I suspect Poppy's not the only one concerned about me."

Grams took a few more steps closer. "Well, no, but she insisted I check on you. Generally, you're the one wide awake and ready to start the day by seven. It's...."

Rhiann picked up her phone. "Yeah, nearly eight, and I should be hitting the road in thirty minutes." She sighed. "Oh, Grams, I nearly blew it last night."

Her grandmother sat on the side of the bed, Poppy still in her arms. "How so?"

"I let Elias kissed me." She looked at Grams. "And I kissed him back. Like *really* kissed him."

Grams smiled. "Well, dear, that's how two people tell each other they're attracted to one another."

Rhiann sighed and slid down among the blankets. "I know that. I haven't been so out of the game I've forgotten ... entirely."

Grams smiled and placed Poppy on the bed. The cat climbed up the far side of the bed and lay down on one of the pillows. As Poppy purred her delight at being on the comfortable piece of furniture, Grams patted Rhiann's arm, still covered by a sheet and blanket.

"I didn't think so. You just seem so upset with yourself – why?" the elderly lady asked.

"You know why. I don't want to feel these things. I don't want to get involved with anyone. There's too much at stake."

"A broken heart?"

Rhiann looked at her grandmother. "Among other things, yes. You know men can't be trusted."

Grams shrugged. "I trusted your grandfather. Your mother trusted your dad. Your sister Erin trusts Daniel."

"See? All the good ones are taken."

Grams chuckled. "I'm sure there are many 'good ones' still out there."

"It's risky, Grams. It's risky to get involved, and after my experiences ...."

Her grandmother's tone sobered. "Honey, love is risky, for both men and women. You need to stop putting your head in the sand. Elias seems like a good man, and you two seem to enjoy yourselves together." Rhiann nodded her head. "Then, my dear, I say 'take a chance.' We have at least two, maybe three months here. If we move to Montana this year or next, there's a chance you can continue seeing him when he visits his mother."

"But what if ...?"

Grams shook her head. Placing two fingers across Rhiann's lips, she said, "None of that. No more living in the past and no more thinking about the future. Enjoy today because we're not promised tomorrow."

Grams smiled. "Now, I'm not saying become a hussy – you deserve better than that."

Rhiann blushed. "Grams ...."

"I mean it. I know what can happen when two people experience sparks. I don't want you to be used nor do I want you to use Elias. Take things slow and if the two of you are meant to be, well, obviously that's wonderful! But if it's not meant to be, I want you to be able to walk out with your dignity and conscious intact. You're a fine lady and you should be treated as such."

Grams stood up. "I'll go get some scrambled eggs going while you get ready for your transport. Can't keep those pups waiting – they've been waiting for new homes long enough!"

"Thanks, Grams."

The older woman smiled. "You're welcome. Just because I'm old and your grandpops has been gone for several years doesn't mean I don't remember being young and feeling passion."

Rhiann smiled and shook her head. "You're something else, Grams."

Her grandmother leaned over and kissed her cheek. "So are you, my sweet. And don't ever let a guy like Brandon tell you, or make you feel, otherwise. By the way, I don't think Elias is like Brandon."

Rhiann's smile remained on her face. "Neither do I."

"I'll see you at breakfast," Grams said. "Want me to take Poppy?"

Rhiann shook her head and reached over to scratch the cat's chin. "No, she can stay. I think I need some cat cuddles."

Grams smiled. "I think you do, too."

After her grandmother left the room, Rhiann reached over and drew the eight-pound cat onto her stomach. Poppy stretched out, and Rhiann tickled the cat's ears, massaging her head and cheeks as well.

"What do you think, Poppy? Is this guy worth the risk?"

The cat simply purred and extended her face for continued ministrations.

"Oh, to be a cat and not worry about such things," Rhiann whispered. "Wanna trade places with me, sweet girl?"

Poppy rubbed her face against Rhiann's hand.

"I didn't think you would," Rhiann commented.

Chapter 12

That afternoon, Rhiann stood by her RAV 4 and watched a burly Native American man load three black dogs into crates in the back of her vehicle. A Hispanic woman stood next to her, reviewing the paperwork on the clipboard.

"This should be all you need," the woman said. "I appreciate you taking the dogs to Tucson and Maricopa for us."

Rhiann smiled at her. "You know it's my pleasure, Rosa. We're in this work together."

"I know," the woman said. "This year, though, has been especially busy, and I hate taking you away from your grandmother so much."

"She has her activities at the resort, and this is my activity. By the way, I told you, didn't I, about the upcoming meeting with the book editor?"

Rosa smiled. "Yes, you did. Seems as if that project must be a go. Congratulations!"

"I don't have a contract yet, but she must like it enough to have me come to her office."

Rosa handed Rhiann the paperwork. "Keep me posted."

"You know I will."

"The dogs are all set, crates and all," the man said, walking over to the two women.

Rhiann held out her hand. "Thanks so much, Joshua. Your help is appreciated."

"Getting the abandoned dogs a second chance is always in our best interest," the 50'ish man replied as he shook her hand. "We're planning a spay/neuter clinic in a few weeks, but I'm sure we'll have some more dogs in need of rescue before then."

Rhiann nodded. "I should be available if you need transport help again."

She shook hands with Rosa. "I'll let you know when I get to Tucson and when I arrive in Maricopa."

"Just a reminder: the dog in the cream-colored coat is Liza and the one in the blue plaid is Logan – they are the Tucson dogs. Angel is the one in the multi-colored coat. The fosters have been told, but just remind them the coats need to stay on the dogs for another week while they heal."

Rhiann shook her head. "Poor things. That must have been a vicious pack of coyotes."

"It was," Joshua said. "Thankfully, they weren't rabid."

"The wounds are healing nicely," Rosa said. "They just need a bit more time."

Rhiann nodded. "Well, time to hit the road. I'll be in touch."

She climbed behind the steering wheel and started the RAV's engine. She pushed the button and the driver's side window came down.

"You both take care. Thanks for all you're doing and for letting me be part of the rescue," she told the pair.

"We appreciate you, Rhiann. Drive safely," Rosa said.

"Thanks. You, too."

Rhiann backed the vehicle from the parking spot, waved at Joshua and Rosa, and headed the RAV toward the highway, away from the rest stop. She glanced back at the crated dogs and said in a soft voice, "You're starting a new chapter of life, my friends, one filled with love and kindness. You'll never be hungry or neglected again."

As the vehicle slipped onto Interstate 10 heading east, Rhiann looked at the landscape. She never tired of the southwest in winter. Red rocks jutting skyward, sandy desert filled with various species of cactus, and an azure sky sparkling with sun. Now that February had rolled in, many cacti bloomed. Shades of red, pink, and white graced the lands she drove past, and the towering, spiny saguaros stood like soldiers guarding the beauty.

Rhiann pushed the 'play' button on the RAV's stereo, and the haunting yet beautiful sounds from Native American flute players. She smiled as the music filled the vehicle.

THREE HOURS LATER, Rhiann stood beside Elias inside his Tucson gallery.

"It's a lovely place," she commented. "You carry beautiful pieces of art."

He smiled. "Thank you. I like to think so." He looked around. "I admit, I'm going to miss this place."

"So you made a decision to sell."

He nodded. "I spoke with a realtor this morning, and she said the market is good for commercial businesses like this. She has a few prospects, one from California and the other from Washington state. I should know something in a few days if either party is interested."

"You'll have opportunity to see your mother more."

He nodded again. "And to travel to Montana."

She noticed he looked at her. "Elias ...."

He held up his hand. "I know. I didn't mean that to pressure you, just stating a fact."

"No, it's not that." Rhiann dropped her voice. "I'm just ... I'm nervous about ... about ...."

"About getting involved?"

She nodded. Elias took her hands into his and drew her into an alcove of the gallery. He glanced around, making sure no one was nearby, and then looked into her eyes. Still clasping her hands, he whispered, "I understand. We'll take things slowly, just as you said last night. I care about you, Rhiann. I respect and admire you. I don't want to lose what we already have for a fling either."

She looked at him, a touch of suspicion in her eyes. He squeezed her hands.

"I mean that. I've been there, done that. Over it, too."

He leaned in and lightly kissed her lips. "Besides, I owe you for finding a great dog for my mom."

Rhiann smiled and relaxed a bit. "Yes, yes you do. How about dinner when I come back to Tucson for my meeting? If your mom stayed with you at your condo that night, Grams and I could get a hotel room and we could all go out to dinner to hopefully celebrate my book contract."

Elias smiled back. "Sounds like a great plan." He leaned closer and whispered in her ear, "But I want to take you out for our own special celebration dinner when I get back to Phoenix. And I know just the right place." He kissed her cheek. "Trust me."

Something in his voice created a red flag warning. She looked at him but nothing in his eyes or expression revealed a concern. A moment later, he said,

"I have those photographs wrapped up and ready to go," he said. "They're in my office."

"I should get the dog out of the car. The Arizona sun can be brutal, even at 65 degrees."

"If you walk the alley between the gallery and the financial planner's office, you'll come to a back parking lot for their office and another small alley to your left. Take that left and you'll see a small patio that connects to the back of the gallery. I'll meet you there."

She nodded and walked through the gallery and outside. Three parking places down waited her RAV 4. Rhiann bee-lined for her vehicle, unlocked it and opened the hatch. A black, greyhound-looking dog eyed her from the travel crate. Rhiann spoke in a low tone, "Hey there, Angel. Want to get out and stretch your legs once more?"

Rhiann opened the kennel door a mite and reached for the dog's orange leash. After wrapping it around her wrist twice, she opened the barred gate wider and allowed the dog to jump onto the pavement. The animal's long, slender legs brought its back to Rhiann's waist. The multi-colored fleece coat helped the black dog stand out. She walked timidly beside Rhiann after the woman locked the RAV again and strolled toward and then down the alley as Elias instructed. She turned left and found him waiting for her. Three wrapped packages graced the mosaic and iron patio table.

Elias smiled at Rhiann and then looked down at the dog next to her. "Nice-looking dog," he commented.

"Her name is Angel," Rhiann responded.

"Is it okay to pet her?"

Rhiann nodded. "Slowly and gently. She's a bit nervous."

Elias squatted and tenderly stroked Angel's side. "Why the coat? It's pretty warm out here."

"Angel and her sibling were attacked by coyotes. They received some extensive wounds, especially to their backs and front quarters. The coats are protecting those wounds as they heal."

"Ah, poor girl!" Elias petted the dog again and then stood up. "Her siblings – are they the dogs you left with a foster family in town?"

Rhiann nodded. "Angel is going to a man who works from home in Maricopa. The rescue I'm helping is hoping that the foster situation might turn into an adoption."

"I hope the same for her. She seems like a nice dog. What breed is she?"

"Hybrid," Rhiann said with a smile. "Likely black lab with some greyhound or whippet and maybe even a bit of Doberman. The lanky look comes from the sighthound side, which greyhounds and whippets are, the black lab, well, that's obvious, and the ears are like a Doberman, except Dobies are generally clipped to keep their ears erect. They are also black of course. All three dogs look almost identical; they're siblings."

Elias looked at her and smiled. "I've learned so much from you these past few days. You have a beautiful heart, Rhiann, an especially kind spirit ... and truthfully, you're incredibly attractive. I am ...I'm quite taken with you; I think you know that."

Rhiann blushed. "I do." She sighed. "I'd be lying if I said I didn't feel the same. But protecting my heart is something I've been doing for quite some time." She sighed and then looked at him. "I think I need to explain my situation a bit more. Can we sit for a few moments?"

Elias nodded and indicated one of the black iron chairs. Rhiann sat down and pulled the dog closer to her feet. Angel lay down on the small brick patio, and Rhiann began to relate her story.

Chapter 13

Rhiann took a deep breath and then, looking at Elias, she said, "Years ago, my fiancé made me choose between and my grandparents at a time when my grandfather became ill. I chose them because they raised my sister and I after our parents died. Him forcing me to choose hurt me badly."

"I can understand," Elias whispered. "What an oaf!"

Rhiann smiled.

"So that experience kept you from dating?" Elias asked.

"I slipped my toes back in the water a few times, but... well, let's just say I think the weirdo door flew open just for me."

A slight smile dawned on Elias' face.

Rhiann took a deep breath and then continued, "I'm not saying you're one of those, and believe me, it's nothing about you. I'm enjoying getting to know you, a lot, really. Grams and I are only here for a few months, though, as you know. I admit, I worry about start something that can't go anywhere because of distance and that might hurt one or both of us. I really don't want my heart to get crushed again."

He nodded. "I understand, Rhiann, really I do." Elias took a deep breath and said, "I was married for fifteen years to a lovely woman. We had two great kids. Then, I lost my job. Everything cratered around me. I lost our house, cars, and ... and my family. She left and took the kids with her."

Rhiann's eyes widened. "Oh, my gosh! I'm so sorry, Elias!"

He gave her a quick smile. "Don't be. My fault."

"It's not your fault the government eliminated your job."

"No, but the gambling and drinking was. So were the get-rich-quick schemes I fell for. My dad helped me get back on my feet. He straightened me out and financed the gallery in Sedona."

"Why there? Why not stay in Montana?"

"I was living in New Mexico at the time. I had picked up my camera again and after making some sales and being able to tuck some money aside, I began travelling and taking pictures. A few galleries in New Mexico carried my art, and one even hosted a show. Dad encouraged me to continue, and after a family trip to the Grand Canyon and seeing how artsy Sedona was, he invested."

"Sounds like he was a great man."

"Yeah, yeah, he was. I wanted to make up for all the harm I caused and be able to help my kids, so I opened my own business, thanks to dad. It did well so I opened another in Phoenix. That's done well, and when Dad passed on, he left me enough to start this gallery. Mom said he knew I wanted to expand and so my inheritance was to help me do just that. I miss that old man of mine a lot at times."

"I can understand. I'm so glad the two of you were close and that he supported your endeavors."

"You told me the other day that you lost your dad and grandfather."

Rhiann nodded. "And my mother."

He closed a hand over hers. "Oh, Rhiann! I'm so sorry."

She looked toward the sky. "My parents died in a car crash when I was sixteen. Grams and Grandpops finished raising me and my sister, and when Grandpops first got sick, I moved back to

Washington to take care of them. My fiancé didn't opt to come with me." Elias tilted his head. "His career was more important than me and my family. He asked me to make a choice – I chose my grandparents."

"We men can be toads sometimes," Elias commented. Rhiann cracked a smile. "So you haven't dated since?"

"No, I gave it a shot a few times. Just more toads."

They chuckled.

Rhiann stood. "Well, Angel and I better get on the highway. She and I still have a trek to get her to her foster dad."

Elias also stood. He picked up the three wrapped packages and said, "I'll carry these to your car."

With Angel beside her, Rhiann walked to the parked RAV 4 next to Elias. Unlocking the vehicle, she said to him, "I appreciate the quick tour and to you listening to me. And understanding."

He placed the artwork behind the front seats, turned, and smiled at her.

"What are friends for?"

Rhiann smiled and then walked Angel to the back of the vehicle. After opening the hatch, she hoisted the dog into the crate.

"You do that so easily," Elias commented.

"Years of practice," she said as she closed the kennel door and the hatch of her vehicle.

Elias smiled at her. "Very dedicated. I wished we had met at earlier in life."

She returned his smile. "We wouldn't be the mature people we are today."

"True, still I feel like I would have fallen madly in love with you." He leaned over and kissed her cheek. "I think I could still fall madly in love with you," he whispered.

Rhiann felt an embarrassed blush mingled a heat of attraction creep up her neck. She smiled and placed a soft hand upon his cheek. Their eyes locked for a moment and then Rhiann said, "Well, Angel and I need hit the road. I know the traffic can get rough this time of day."

Elias reached into the back pocket of his black jeans. He pulled out his wallet and handed Rhiann two twenty-dollar bills.

"For gas and a quick dinner," he said. "I promise the meal we share together will be much classier."

"Oh, Elias, I don't need this," Rhiann protested. "I was passing through here anyway and I have food money. It's part of the dog transporting thing."

"I insist. You're doing me a favor, saving me time, and you need to go into downtown Phoenix. That's worth hazard pay."

Elias grinned, and she followed suit.

"Are you sure?" Rhiann asked.

He nodded. "Very. Take it."

She acquiesced. "Thank you. I appreciate it. I'll donate to the rescue – they can use additional funds."

He peeled two more twenties from his wallet. "Add this to whatever you don't want to use." She stared at him, and he placed the bills into her hand. "I insist. What you told me about these reservation dogs, I want to help. And I'll donate more in the future."

Rhiann shook her head. A wave of passion mixed with appreciation came over her and she pulled his head to her face and kissed him with fervor. When their lips parted, Elias said, as if in a daze, "Wow. If that's a benefit for donating to dog rescue, I'll definitely be giving more."

Rhiann grinned and in essence skipped to the driver's side of the RAV. She unlocked the door and climbed in behind the wheel. Elias held it open as Rhiann laid her shoulder-strapped red and gray purse on the passenger seat. She leaned toward the glovebox and deposited Elias' money there. As she began to straighten back up, he grabbed her waist and pulled her to him. He kissed her with vigor. After lingering his lips on hers, Elias whispered, "Two can play that game."

Rhiann didn't respond. Elias grinned and closed her door. She started the RAV and lowered the window.

"Thanks again for adding my artwork to your transport," Elias said.

"After I drop Angel off with her foster dad in Maricopa, I'll head over immediately."

"You remember how to get there, right?"

She smiled and pointed to the RAV's GPS. "Still locked in."

"Call me if you have any problems."

Rhiann frowned. "What kind of problems might I have?"

"Car trouble, out of gas, getting lost, things like that. I don't expect you'd have any other problems."

"I'll not have any problems. I'm trying to think more like Grams."

He smiled. "Atta girl."

"You're sure someone will be at the gallery?"

Elias nodded. "Evan knows you'll arrive after hours. Just call the number I gave you earlier – he'll have the business line forwarded to his cell phone if he's grabbing a bite to eat."

"Okay, well," she said, a smile on her face. "I'll see you sometime soon."

"That you will," he said in a quiet tone. "Drive safely."

Rhiann nodded and pulled her vehicle out of the parking place onto the street. She gave Elias a small wave of her hand, and he returned the gesture. Rhiann pointed the RAV toward the interstate, thoughts and emotions awhirl.

Chapter 14

Ninety-minutes later Rhiann pulled her vehicle off the interstate and onto the parking lot of a small rest area. After stopping the RAV and shutting down the engine, she remained in the driver's seat for a few moments.

She shook her head, smiled, and touched her lips with her fingers. *Well, this is certainly what I'd planned. Maybe Grams is right – maybe it is time for me to pull my head out of the sand. Elias is charming, intelligent, interested, and certainly easy on the eyes. Definitely NOT Class A boring.*

Rhiann lighted from the vehicle, taking in the evening view. The western sky hues whispered to her heart, casting a rosy glow to the horizon and shadowy light upon the desert landscape. Saguaros stood like soldiers in formation, ancient arms curled with strength by eons of endurance. Wrens flitted between the tall cacti, adding music to the evening.

"A good time for a walk," Rhiann murmured.

She opened the RAV's hatch and helped Angel from the crate and from the vehicle. As the woman and dog meandered around the pavement, Rhiann's thoughts once again became a jumbled mess. Her brain kept reasoning the 'why' of not getting romantically involved with Elias, while her heart tried to convince her even a few months in the company of the businessman and artist would be enjoyable.

She sat on a concrete bench under a wooden covering and watched the sun dip below the horizon. Shades of rose, apricot, and blueberry spread across the vast sky. Angel leaned against Rhiann's knee, and the woman slid from the bench onto the concrete pad. Sitting beside the dog, Rhiann wrapped an arm across the canine's shoulder.

"Life deals us strange cards sometimes, uh, Angel? You have no idea what's happening and yet you trust me to take care of you. I have no idea what lies ahead for my future, and yet, I trust Grams to help us get to where we're supposed to go. I can't trust my own heart because of the past. Yet, here you are, trusting Rosa, Joshua, me, and a person neither of us have met yet. Perhaps we humans need to be more like dogs – trust and have faith that things work out for good."

Rhiann sighed and hugged the dog close. Her cell phone, tucked into her khaki's right pocket, pinged. Rhiann removed the device and brought up the text message.

CHECK YOUR EMAIL ASAP. I HAVE TO POSTPONE OUR MEETING NEXT WEEK DUE TO A FAMILY EMERGENCY. I'LL RESCHEDULE WITH YOU IN A FEW WEEKS, DEPENDING ON HOW LONG I'M GONE. BOOK DEAL IN THE WORKS. CONGRATULATIONS AND HAPPY TO HAVE YOU ABOARD! – ANGELA HOLT, FLOWERING DESERT PUBLISHING

"Oh, my gosh!" Rhiann said aloud.

A large grin grew on her face. Her fingers played with the apps on her phone until she brought up her email account. She scanned the note Angela had sent, and her smile grew larger. She pumped her fist in the air and said, "Yes!"

She hugged Angel, the dog, against her body. "I get to share your story, and the stories of the other reservation dogs, with the world! The door has opened, Angel, and by golly, we're going to walk through it!"

A wave of gratitude washed over her. Rhiann sat next to Angel as tears enveloped her eyes. The pup with her southwestern-designed coat covering the surgical scars and coyote bite marks raised its head and licked Rhiann's face. She hugged Angel closer. The woman and dog sat in peaceful silence and watched the sunset's colors dilute across the sky.

THREE HOURS LATER, Rhiann pulled the RAV into the parking area near her grandmother's cottage at the resort. She stepped out of the vehicle, stretched her arms and torso, and looked at the now-darkened sky. A half-moon shone, radiating light in the parking area. Mingled with the still-lit-for-Christmas lights, Magnifico shone like early morning.

Rhiann removed her cell phone from her purse and scrolled her contact list. Once she found his name, she punched the lettering. After four rings, Elias picked up.

"Hi, there, Rhiann. I take it you're back at the resort, safe and well?"

"Yes, I made it back. Angel is with her foster dad and your photographs are at the gallery." She took a deep breath. "Elias, something about that guy who met me, your employee, Evan I believe you said his name was?"

"Yes. What about him, Rhiann?"

"He was incredibly rude, asking me all kinds of questions like if I'd looked inside the wrapping, if I saw you placing the photographs into the packaging, and other things that just didn't set right with me."

"Oh, I'm sorry! He's finicky about the art we bring in, and since he doesn't know you ... I apologize for the third-degree treatment."

"You did tell him I was coming, didn't you?"

"Yes, yes, I told him. Perhaps he was grumpy because I asked you to drop the pictures off and it was late. I've asked him to stay later a few times, and he's always been okay with the request, and he didn't say anything different to me when I asked him this time. Might have had a bad day or something. Again, I apologize."

Rhiann sighed. "Well, I'm tired, too, so maybe I interpreted things I shouldn't have. I'm sorry I bothered you about it."

"No, that's quite all right. I'll speak to him when I'm back in Phoenix in the next few days."

"No, don't bother. You're likely right. Everybody can have an off day. I was rattled from the traffic as well and had a difficult time finding a parking place, so I was likely super-sensitive. Let's just forget it. I did want you to know, though, that the transport and drop-off went well and that your photographs are now with Evan."

"Thanks again, Rhiann. I appreciate your help.

A grin came to her face. "I do have some great news to share."

"I can't wait to hear it."

"I officially have a book contract!"

"Excellent! I knew that would come through. Congratulations!"

"Thanks. Sadly, the publisher had to postpone our meeting due to a family emergency, so it looks like I won't be making the trip to Tucson with Grams and your mother for a while."

"Well, when you have that all lined up, let me know and I'll make sure I have the entire day off. We'll spend the day together."

"I'd like that. Well, I need to unwind from the trip, so I'll say good night."

"Good night, Rhiann. I look forward to seeing you again very soon. Sleep well."

"You, too, Elias. Thank you."

Rhiann heard Elias click off and she did as well. She locked the RAV and walked to Grams' cottage.

Chapter 15

After unlocking the door, Rhiann stepped inside and called out, "Hey, Grams! I'm back."

Her grandmother looked over the top of the book she was reading as she sat in one of the living room's burgundy recliners. She smiled and said, "Welcome back, dear. How was the traffic downtown?"

Rhiann flopped on the toffee-colored couch.

"A nightmare! I hope I never have to do that again! What goes on during a Tuesday night in February in Phoenix?"

"Ah, spring training?"

"I thought that began next week."

"I watched the news tonight and heard some of the teams came in early. Maybe open batting practice."

"Well, it's something. I think there were more cars on the freeway than I've seen in the past few winters around here."

"More snowbirders, most likely as well as the baseball teams," Grams commented. "People do continue to get older."

Rhiann sighed. "Tell me about it."

Grams studied her closely. "Are you all right, dear?"

Rhiann smiled and sat up. "Tired is all. I have some news, some great news."

Her grandmother's face lit up. "The book?" Rhiann nodded with excitement. "You got the contract!"

Rhiann nodded her head vigorously. "I'm going to be an author! An author that helps rescue groups!"

She stood up, pulled her cell phone from her purse, and walked toward her grandmother. She bent down beside the elderly woman and opened her photo file. Pictures of Angel and the other two dogs as well as group shots appeared, and as she shared the eight photos with Grams, she explained the dogs' plight, injuries, and hope for forever homes. She also showed Grams two photos of Joshua and Rosa.

"These are the people I'm dedicating the book to," Rhiann explained. "Rosa and Joshua introduced me to the world of reservation dog rescue. They work with the tribes to help the strays and to bring low-cost spay/neuter and vaccination clinics to the reservations. I've interviewed them for articles and for the book."

"That's fine work they do," Grams commented.

Rhiann nodded her head. "Not easy work either. With the stories I've been able to publish, though, they've received increased donations and additional veterinarian help. Their programs have more funding now than ever, so more dogs and more Native families, are helped."

Grams smiled and patted Rhiann's arm. "That's wonderful, dear! Your writing and your rescue work are doing so much good for so many. And now I get to say my granddaughter is an author. I'm quite proud of you!"

Rhiann kissed her grandmother's cheek. "Thanks, Grams. I really appreciate your encouragement."

"And when we get to Montana, you'll be able to do even more! I received a call today from a realtor friend of Helen's – she has a few properties she thinks can work for what we're wanting to do.

We wouldn't be far from Helen, and if Elias came to visit, you could see him as well."

Rhiann sat on the arm of the chair her grandmother occupied. "Grams, I took some time to think about Elias. Now that I have a book contract, I'm going to have a lot of work ahead of me. I can't manage a writing career and authoring a book and taking care of us, especially if we do find something in Montana to buy, plus setting up a sanctuary, all the while trying to maintain a romantic relationship."

Rhiann shook her head. "I just can't do all of that. I choose to give up romantic involvement, with Elias or anyone else, until the book is done at a minimum. I talked with Elias after dropping off the two dogs being fostered in Tucson. I explained a bit about what happened with Brandon and how I've kept myself out of the dating arena for the most part and why. Tomorrow, or whenever next I see Elias, I'll tell him how I need to focus on my writing career, especially with this book deal, and also focus on taking care of you ..."

"I don't want to be the reason you take yourself out of the dating game all together. Elias seems like a wonderful man ..."

"So did Brandon, and I learned five years later how selfish, conceited, and controlling he was," Rhiann responded. "I don't want to do that again, Grams, you know that."

Her grandmother didn't reply. Rhiann rose and said, "It's been a long day. I'm going to take a shower, read a bit, and go to bed. Do you need anything right now?" Grams shook her head. "Oh, by the way, our trip to Tucson and the desert museum is postponed a week or two. The publisher had an emergency in her family and she'll get in touch with me about rescheduling. But it's going to be awhile."

"Helen will be disappointed."

"It's just a postponement. You and she will be able to visit his gallery there in a few weeks. I have to say – it's very lovely."

Rhiann started down the hallway to the bathroom nearest her bedroom. Poppy, the cat, lay stretched in the hallway. Rhiann stopped to scratch the aging cat's tummy.

"How was your day, sweet kitty?" Rhiann murmured. "Tomorrow, we'll sit out on the veranda and enjoy the 70-degree day, how's that sound?"

The purr that resonated from the Persian mix caused Rhiann to smile.

"You always say the sweetest things, Poppy-girl."

Rhiann continued her walk to the bathroom and shut the door.

Chapter 16

The next morning, as Rhiann created breakfast in the kitchen, her cell phone rang. She looked at the screen, and as Elias' cell number popped into view, she smiled as she answered.

"Good morning, gallery owner. How are you?"

She sensed his smile over the phone. "I'm well. How about you? Did you get much sleep last night?"

"After getting lost in Maricopa twice, and in downtown Phoenix three times, and then trying to find a parking place, encountering Evan, and then figuring out how to get back to Cave Creek, yes, I did get some sleep."

"I'm sorry you had trouble getting around. Downtown can be crazy, especially at night when the ball teams are settling in, and when you're not used to the area. I do appreciate you getting those art pieces to my gallery."

"You've said that several times, and you're still welcome," she said with a slight laugh.

"I want you to know I had a talk earlier with Evan," Elias said. "He admitted to being grumpy and a bit put out staying later. He asked me to extend his apologies to you. I told him to be honest with me next time and let me know if it's inconvenient to stay later when I ask. Seems I ruined a special dinner his girlfriend had lined up, so I'm sending them to The Lustre Rooftop Bar tomorrow night on me. He's ecstatic and said his girlfriend would be, too."

"I've heard about that place – sounds swanky."

"Maybe we could go sometime. In fact, that's where we should go to celebrate your book contract. How's Saturday night? I close the gallery at five-thirty so I could set reservations for six."

Rhiann chewed her lower lip. "Elias, I ... I need to tell you something. I've come to a decision. With the book deal and my other writing, I'm going to be slammed with work and I'm going to need to concentrate. I have Grams to care for and the pet rescue work I volunteer with. I can't ... I can't get involved romantically ... as much as ... as much as we both may want that, I just can't. I'm sorry."

Silence greeted her for a few moments. Nervously, she remarked, "Elias? Elias, are you there?"

"Yeah, I'm here. I'm sort of stunned, but I hear you."

"I'm sorry. I do want us to be friends. We started out that way, can we just continue?"

"Sure. Well, I guess I'll see you sometime when I'm at the resort."

"I hope so. I do like you, Elias, and perhaps, as you said, if we'd met at another time... well, I appreciate you're understanding."

"Goodbye, Rhiann."

He hung up. She stared at her phone and whispered, "Goodbye, Elias."

She turned off the cell phone and returned to ready breakfast. She heard a sound in the living room and walked over to peer into the room. Grams, with Poppy trotting beside her, walked toward her.

"Did I hear you on the phone a moment ago?" Grams asked.

Rhiann nodded. "I was talking with Elias."

"And?" Grams asked, sliding out a kitchen chair.

"And I told him I couldn't see him, not romantically anyway. I let him know I just can't juggle everything that's going on and a relationship, but that I still wanted us to be friends."

"What did he say to that?"

Rhiann sighed. "What most men say when you tell them that."

"I'm sorry, sweetie. I was really rooting for the two of you."

Rhiann shrugged. "This is a reason to never become involved with a man."

Grams looked at Rhiann as she made the statement, "You're disappointed."

"Trying not to be, but yeah, I am a little."

Rhiann stepped away and then came back with two cups of coffee, which she set on the table. She pulled out a chair and sat next to her grandmother.

"He thanked me again for bringing the art pieces to his Phoenix gallery. Said he talked with his employee and that it was all a misunderstanding. Still, there's something about that guy ... his employee ...."

"Evan, right?"

Rhiann nodded her head. "I felt ... uncomfortable around him, like there was something ... mafia-like about him." Rhiann shrugged. "Likely just my weariness and jitters, being downtown by myself around all those people."

"Another reason to like Montana – less people than around here, that's for sure."

Rhiann attempted to shake the sadness she felt at likely losing Elias' friendship. She pasted on a smile and asked, "So, did you and Helen find a property for us to look into?"

"Possibly two," Grams responded. "When you have a few minutes, you can look them up on the computer. I have the realtor's web address and the listing number of the properties."

Grams picked up her coffee cup and sipped the hot liquid. She looked at Rhiann over the rim of the mug.

"Are you sure about not dating Elias?"

Rhiann looked at her grandmother. "Grams, please don't push this. I have too much to focus on, too much to do. I can't be distracted from my work and my goals. Or from taking care of you."

"I think it's too bad. I like the guy," Grams said.

Rhiann sighed and looked out the sliding patio door. Poppy had moved from inside the cottage and now was lounging in the morning sun, laying on her back as the rays of warmth covered her tummy.

"Well, he's not a weirdo and not a toad," Rhiann said. "This would be easier if he was." She sighed. "I want to focus on what I'm doing well, Grams, and that's my writing and rescue endeavors. I don't want complications."

Grams looked at her and responded, "You certainly take care of me well."

Rhiann smiled. "That's what matters."

Chapter 17

Later that morning, Rhiann sat on the veranda, laptop perched on her knees as she reclined in a lawn chair. Poppy now rested in the shade, her round head atop her front paws. Rhiann's cell phone vibrated on the wicker table nearby. She reached for it and checked the caller ID. She frowned and then answered.

"Hello, this is Rhiann Kelly."

"Rhiann, this is Etta Johannsen from *Big Sky Magazine*."

"Etta! Hello! This is a surprise."

"I know I usually email, but I'm leaving for a long weekend in a few hours, and I decided it's just easier to pick up the phone and call. Are you still in Arizona?"

"Yes. My grandmother and I generally stay until the at least the first of April, oftentimes the middle. Why?"

"Good! Because you can do the interviews you need."

"Interviews?"

"Yes. I love your idea of talking to snowbirds and comparing them with the migration of sandhill cranes. I want you to do interviews with people in the area you and your grandmother are staying and I want you to go to Bosque del Apache National Wildlife Refuge in New Mexico and interview a biologist there. The story about the moose and sandhill cranes near Yellowstone is coming together well, and we plan to publish it in the summer issue. We can publish your snowbird story in the fall, but we have an opening for the spring edition – a story we'd planned on fell through – so I'd like to run that story in the spring issue. But you'll have to work fast. Deadline is March 10."

Rhiann sucked in a breath. "That's not far off."

"We'll pay extra since it's last minute and of course we'll pay you for photos. Your proposal came at just the right time and the topic is relevant for spring. Take it from the angle of returning north. Can you do that?"

"Yes. I'll get on it right away."

"Can you drive to the refuge next week? I understand the cranes begin their northern migration the middle of February. If you could go this week, even better."

"I don't think I can this week, as I already have a few appointments, but I'll call the headquarters today and see what I can set up for next week. Or perhaps I can go on Saturday if a biologist will be around."

"Great! Even though I'll be out of the office, I'll have my cell phone with me and I'll be checking emails periodically. Let me know if you run into any snags. I'll send you a contact for the story, photos, travel, and last-minute assignment. You'll have it within the hour."

"Thanks so much, Etta!"

"Oh, no, thank you, Rhiann. I'm looking forward to working with you more in the future. You produce quality work, and that's what we're about at this publication. I'll be in touch."

The editor hung up, and, with a smile and a chuckle, Rhiann did the same.

"Well, that's amazing!"

"What is dear?" Grams asked, stepping onto the patio.

"I just received a call from Etta, the managing editor of *Big Sky Magazine*. She likes my story idea of snowbirders and sandhill cranes, and she wants the story before mid-March."

"Oh, my! That's fast. Can you make that deadline?"

"Of course – I'm a McCallister-Kelly woman, aren't I?"

Grams smiled as she sat next to her granddaughter. "That you are. You are strong, capable, intelligent, diligent, and have so many other positive qualities."

Rhiann smiled. "Thanks, Grams. I get those from you, Grandpops, and Dad."

"Your mother, too. She may not have been full Irish, but she had many positive qualities as well, and blending those Finnish traits with your Irish roots created the person you are and the person Erin is, and they are both wonderful!"

The smile remained on Rhiann's face. "You've always been so encouraging, Grams. I do love you."

Rhiann reached over and kissed her grandmother's cheek. She noticed tears glistening in Grams' eyes.

"I love you, too, child, so very much!"

LATER THAT AFTERNOON, Rhiann sat at the kitchen table, her fingers pounding the keyboard of her laptop. Her phone pinged that she had received a text. She saved the document she was creating on the computer and checked her message.

HEY, SIS! GOT YOUR MESSAGE ABOUT THE BOOK CONTRACT. CONGRATULATIONS! I'LL CALL WHEN DANIEL AND I GET BACK. WE TOOK AN EARLY VALENTINE VACATION TO THE BAHAMAS TO CELEBRATE OUR ANNIVERSARY. DANIEL'S PARTENTS ARE

CARING FOR THE KIDS. ALL IS WELL. I'M PROUD OF YOU! TALK SOON. LOVE TO YOU AND GRAMS. – ERIN

Rhiann chuckled. Grams stepped into view from the living room.

"What is it, dear? Is everything okay?"

Rhiann looked up from her text with a smile. "Erin texted. She and Daniel are in the Bahamas for an anniversary trip."

"Ah, good – I'm glad they got to go. I take it Daniel's parents are taking care of Brittany and Brian?"

Rhiann nodded. "Erin seems pleased about the book deal."

"And why wouldn't she be? We're all proud of you, dear."

Thanks, Grams. I wonder if we could get Erin, Daniel, and the kids out here during the kids' spring break? It would be great to see them."

"Yes, it would. You should suggest that to her. We could all go to the Grand Canyon."

"Or to Best Friends. I know Brittany would enjoy that," Rhiann said.

"Not sure the rest of the family would," commented Grams.

"Erin would," Rhiann protested. "She loved the animals on the farm, and the pets we had growing up."

"She didn't care much for that billy goat we had, if I remember correctly. Although that goat didn't care much for most people either."

Rhiann grinned. "He could be a cranky guy, that's for sure. Let's plan to call Erin after she and Daniel get back and invite them and the kids over here before we leave to drive back north."

Grams nodded. "Good plan. It's been too long since we've seen them." She shook her head. "I bet I wouldn't even recognize my great-grandchildren!"

Just then, the phone in the cottage rang. Rhiann walked over and glanced at the caller ID. Recognizing the call as from coming on-site, Rhiann answered.

"Hello, this is Rhiann, Martha Kelly's granddaughter."

"Oh, Rhiann! I'm so scared!"

"Hello? Who is this?"

"Helen Griffin. It's bad, Rhiann, really bad."

"What, Helen? What's bad? Are you hurt?"

She glanced at her grandmother, whose face took on a look of concern.

"My heart is broken! My Elias, my dear son, has been arrested!"

"What? Arrested? For what?"

"Drugs. They say he sells drugs! That can't be, not my Elias!"

Rhiann stared out the window, unable to respond. *Elias? Drugs? Could it be true?*

"I need a ride to the jail. I can't drive, I don't know this area. I have to see my son!"

"Try to calm down, Helen. How did you get this news?"

"Elias called me. He told me everything, and he said I should call my daughter in El Paso. But I just can't because I can't believe this. Not my boy."

"Did he say where he's at, what jail? Which community?"

"Scottsdale. They picked him up on his way back to the gallery downtown."

"Back from where? I thought he was in Tucson."

"I don't know. Maybe he came back to the Phoenix gallery. He didn't say. I'm just a wreck!"

Rhiann looked at her grandmother, who was frowning and had a concerned expression on her face. Rhiann shrugged.

"Grams and I will be over to your place soon. Try to calm down."

She heard Helen crying. "I can't. This is my boy, my Elias. Surely the police have made a mistake!" More tears and sniffles. "He's been locked up for nearly three hours. I need to get there – I need to bail him out. Can you take me?"

"Of course I can. Mrs. Griffin, I think we need more information. First, we need to make sure that's where Elias really is. Secondly, can he be bailed out if he is in jail? And thirdly, how much bail money is needed if he can be? Let me make some calls, and I'll let you know what I find out. Okay?"

"Okay, yes. I guess so. I'm just so distraught, I don't know right from left."

"Totally understandable. I'll call you back soon."

Rhiann hung up and leaned against the wall of the room.

"What is it, honey?" Grams asked. "Is Helen all right?"

Rhiann looked at her grandmother. "Slight change of plans for Friday, Grams, and you're not going to believe this."

Chapter 18

Later that night, Grams and Rhiann sat at their dining room table drinking tea.

"You said this was chamomile, right? Because we're going to need it," Grams said.

"Yes, it's chamomile, and yes, I chose it specifically to help us sleep."

"I just can't believe that Elias Griffin has been a drug smuggler for nearly a decade," Grams said. "Poor Helen!"

"At least he's owning up to his crime and not dragging his family through hell."

"His mother is already going through hell," Grams said. "I imagine his sister is as well."

"Helen said her daughter will arrive later tonight."

"I wish she would have let us bring her back here. I'm afraid for her – she shouldn't be alone in that hotel room, waiting for her daughter," Grams said.

"I know – I felt the same way. But she has Holly, so she's not completely alone. Her daughter's flight from El Paso arrives in Phoenix soon, so that helps."

Grams shook her head. "Still, I feel terrible for her."

"So do I." Rhiann sighed. "I never suspected this of Elias. And to think – I carried packages for him!"

Grams studied Rhiann. "Do you think you'll have to go to court and testify?"

She shook her head. "Since he's pled guilty, there won't be a trial." She shuddered. "But if he hadn't of fessed up and took responsibility ... I might have been in a heap of trouble, even though I didn't knowingly do anything."

Rhiann and her grandmother looked at each other, thinking about what could have happened. They sipped their tea for a few moments in silence.

"Would you ever do anything like that to fund your dreams?" Grams asked. "I mean, I would hope not, but, well, I wouldn't have thought Elias would either. Didn't he tell you the inheritance he received funded his business at start-up?"

"Yes, he did say that, and no, Grams, I'd never do anything of the sort. If so, I would have started an animal sanctuary years ago," Rhiann said with a wavering smile. "Besides, I was engaged to a cop, remember? I couldn't have broken the law."

Rhiann's smile wavered. Each woman took another taste of tea. Afterward, Rhiann added, "I'm perfectly content to maintain my writing career and to be a transporter for rescue. If my dream for an animal sanctuary never happens, that's okay. It's a dream, not an obsession."

"My hope is for your dream to come true. You have a beautiful heart, Rhiann, and you have the courage and perseverance to make that dream come true. I plan to help you. We'll do it – together."

Rhiann reached over and clasped her grandmother's hand. "I love you, Grams."

"And I love you, child, more than you'll ever know."

Rhiann sighed and then stood. She picked up Poppy, who lay in another chair, and she cuddled the cat close to her chest.

"What's on your mind, dear girl?" Grams asked, watching Rhiann.

"I was starting to fall for Elias."

Grams nodded. "I know, and I believe he truly felt something for you."

Rhiann shuddered. "Just think what vat of doo-doo I'd have been in if I'd taken those extra steps."

"You made a wise decision to not get romantically involved with him. Your intuition serves you well," Grams said.

"I guess he was a toad after all."

Rhiann cuddled Poppy against her face.

"No, dear, I don't think so." Rhiann looked at her grandmother. "Elias was a man desperate to maintain his image and his business. Happens to the best of people sometimes, no matter their gender."

Rhiann nodded and responded, "You're probably right."

She set Poppy back down in a chair, picked up her mug of tea, and drank the warm liquid. As Rhiann sat down at the table again, she said, "I'm glad we'll be going to Bosque del Apache in a few days. Seeing the cranes and doing interviews will help keep my mind off what's happened."

"Poor Helen!" Grams said, shaking her head. "I'm so glad her daughter can get here so quickly."

"I truly hope, Grams, this is the last of the excitement in our lives for a while."

Grams patted Rhiann's hand. "Let's focus on the good kind of excitement – your book and your new article. When we get to New Mexico, we'll celebrate and put all this behind us."

A small smile came to Rhiann's face. "That's an excellent idea. A margarita sounds rather good right now."

Grams chuckled. “I agree! Maybe we should ditch this tea and hit the bar!”

Rhiann laughed, and Grams joined in.

Chapter 19

A few weeks later, Rhiann sat by the pool, basking in the mid-morning Arizona sun. She reviewed the article on the screen of her laptop, crinkling her face as she concentrated on the sentences. She moved her fingers across the keyboard, deleting words and replacing them with others. She saved the changes, relaxed against the lounge chair, and smiled.

"That's the look I prefer to see on my granddaughter's face."

Rhiann looked up, the smile still vivid. Her grandmother stood beside her.

"You must be happy with the article now," Grams said.

"I am. I think the magazine editor will be, too. I'm so grateful to the Chapmans and Grishams for sharing their stories. I wish it could have worked out to include Helen."

"Well, with her son now in prison and Helen now living with her daughter in Texas, the story wouldn't have come together at all," Grams said. "At least you found Doris Clemons to add insight as a first-time snowbirder."

"Absolutely true. And to think she helps the Glendale Animal Shelter! Another rescue contact!"

She drank from the iced tea glass on the nearby table and then said, "I feel sorry for Helen – what a thing to deal with! I'm glad she has her daughter, and I'm certainly glad I didn't have to do anything but give a statement."

Grams nodded and sat in a nearby chair.

"I was worried he'd drag you into the trial since you transported those photographs and frames for him." She shook her head. "Smuggling drugs through his artwork – clever, yet stupid at the same time."

"With a guilty plea, at least his family is spared the longevity of a trial," Rhiann said. "Hopefully, Helen and her daughter can move on."

"Speaking of moving on, how are you doing?" Grams inquired. "Now you have the article about done and the book to start. By the way, I enjoyed meeting your editor the other day, and I'm glad all the details of the book contract were worked out. I'm wondering how you're feeling about all this?"

Rhiann grinned. "How do you think? I'm so jazzed! And grateful."

She stood up and stretched. "I just have to remember to move a bit more. I can become so engrossed in what I'm doing on the computer, I lose track of time. Are you going for a walk, Grams?"

"I thought a stroll around the grounds would be nice before lunch."

"Mind if I join you?"

Grams smiled and stood. "That's why I stopped by. I was hoping you would, but I wasn't sure you'd be at a good ending point."

Rhiann leaned down and closed her laptop. "Well, I am." She slipped on the sandals next to the cushioned chair. "I'll be emailing the story tonight, and then I'm taking a break for a few days before tackling the book. Maybe we could take time and head up to Best Friends since Erin and her family don't have time when they visit in two weeks?"

"That sounds just lovely. We can take in Zion and Bryce Canyon national parks as well," Grams responded. "We haven't been to those places in a few years."

Rhiann slipped her arm through her grandmother's, and the two women strolled from the pool area toward a paved pathway connecting the resort to a nearby open space.

"We'll need to check the weather report and make sure no snowstorms are forecast," Rhiann said.

"Do you have transports or adoptions to help with this week?"

Rhiann shook her head. "No, I told everyone I needed some time to write and to spend with you and with Erin and her family when they come."

"Well, if someone needs a transport north and the weather does cooperate to go to Best Friends, we could always take a needy animal along. Or when we take Erin, Daniel, and the kids to the Grand Canyon. "

Rhiann smiled and squeezed her grandmother's arm. "You love this rescue work as much as I do, I think!"

Grams smiled back. "Well, why shouldn't I? I love animals, too, you know."

Rhiann craned her neck and kissed her grandmother's cheek. "Peas in a pod, you and me."

"Except when it comes to living in Montana. You haven't been as engaged looking at property as I would have thought by now."

"I've been busy, Grams."

They stopped walking. The older woman took her granddaughter's hands into her own. She spoke in a quiet yet firm voice.

"Rhiann, none of us know how much time we have, and at my age, that reality sets in deep. You want to create an animal sanctuary; I want to help you do that. I want to return to Montana. All three can happen. There's nothing in Washington for me anymore, sweetheart. I was born in Montana, and I'd like to die there."

"Grams, you're not going to die ..."

"Of course I will, dear. Not today, maybe not tomorrow, but one day, and I'd like to be back home."

"You have all your friends, all of our neighbors in Spokane. Grandpops is buried in Spokane. You don't know anyone in Montana. Neither do I."

"We know Helen," Grams retorted. "People in Montana are very friendly, very welcoming. If we bought a small parcel of land, you could open the animal sanctuary you've been dreaming of, just like the one at Best Friends. I know want to do it."

"Land is expensive, Grams. Neither of us can afford to purchase property there, at least not in an area we need."

"I haven't said anything about this but now is a good time. Your grandpops and I sold the farm for a good price, and I've been saving that. With what I could get for the house, we could buy some acreage, at least enough to have a small sanctuary."

"You used the farm money to buy the Spokane house, Grams."

A small smile came to the older woman's face as the two stopped walking.

"Not all of it. And don't forget I get Grandpops' pension. We can do this, dear."

Rhiann frowned. "How much money are we talking, Grams?"

Her grandmother's smile remained. "Enough."

Rhiann sighed and shook her head as they resumed walking. "You're keeping things from me, and I'm not sure I like that."

"I still have a good mind, and I have a good financial planner. You have enough to deal with, so don't fret."

"I really don't have to have an animal sanctuary, Grams. It's a dream but one that may not be meant to be."

Her grandmother pulled on Rhiann's arm, and the women stopped walking again.

"It is meant to be," Grams said, looking directly into Rhiann's eyes. "We just haven't found the right place yet,"

The granddaughter's face crinkled in thought.

"Aw, there's that thinking look again," Grams said. "What's stirring in your brain now?"

"Back taxes."

Grams' eyes remained fixed on Rhiann's. "What? No, we're not behind on the taxes. They're not due until May."

"No, Grams, not the Spokane house taxes."

Rhiann clasped her grandmother's hands as an excited look dawned her on face. "We could look at properties with back taxes due. Or foreclosed property and parcels being auctioned. Those are some ways we might be able to buy land in Montana, a parcel large enough for a sanctuary."

A big grin graced Grams' face. "Yes! What a great idea, Rhiann!" She sobered a moment. "Although sadly, at the loss to someone else."

"That's true, but if you really want to move to Montana and if you want to try to get property, this would be the route to go. The owner losing the land would know good people would cherish the property, take excellent care of it, and use it for a good purpose."

"True enough. Well, my precious granddaughter, I say we have lunch, you finish that article and get it sent off, and then we get on that computer of yours to start looking!"

Rhiann grinned. "Yes, ma'am!"

They turned back toward the resort.

Chapter 20

As Rhiann and Grams sat in the resort's restaurant, salads in front of them, Grams said to her granddaughter, "We can check the weather report and see if we can make our trip to southern Utah and stay at Best Friends for a few days. Maybe you can talk with some of the staff members about setting up your sanctuary. I remember you telling me they offer courses and trainings."

Rhiann laughed and squeezed her grandmother's arm. "They do. Keep in mind, though, Grams, we may not find what we want or need in Montana right away."

"All the more reason to start now. We can check every few days for new listings for property with back taxes owed. The sooner we start and continue looking, the more opportunity we have in finding what suits us."

Grams' grin widened, and she clapped her hands. "Oh! Wouldn't it be wonderful if we found something close to where I grew up?!"

As they journeyed toward the resort's restaurant, Rhiann asked, "That was western Montana, wasn't it, Grams?"

"Southwestern actually. Near a town called Colter, about forty miles from Bozeman."

"That's right. I bet the area has changed a lot since you were there."

"Oh, it has!" Rhiann looked at her. Grams shrugged. "I've been checking in on the area now and then during the past few years."

Rhiann stopped and stared into her grandmother's eyes. "You've been plotting this for a while, haven't you?"

Grams shrugged again. "Thinking about it the past two or three years, yes. Since your grandpops passed, I've felt this longing to return to the area where I was born. Spokane has never really felt like home. I loved the farm, don't get me wrong, but the city ..." She shook her head. "I'm a country girl at heart. Even though I lived in Boise when I met Grandpops, I never really wanted to stay. I was thankful when we moved, but sad we had to spend so much time in or near cities. When he retired and found that little farm outside of Spokane, that was our compromise – acreage but near a large town for medical purposes in our older age."

"What about now, Grams? Montana doesn't have large cities."

"I know, and I'm glad. If we found something outside of Missoula, like Helen did, or better yet, outside of Bozeman, both towns have good healthcare services; that would work fine. Remember what Helen said."

Rhiann nodded and then said, "Don't you want to be buried next to Grandpops? I thought you purchased a plot for yourself after he died."

Her grandmother nodded. "I did. But where one is buried, does that really matter? Neither he nor I will know." Rhiann pondered that statement. "I can sell the plot if we find the right place in Montana. Being laid to rest near my parents would be fine with me."

They finished their walk back to the resort.

"Why don't you find us a nice place to sit outside here and I'll let the hostess know where we are and bring out two menus? We'll eat lunch at the resort instead of at our villa," Grams said.

"You should sit down and let me do all that," Rhiann said.

The older woman shook her head with a smile. "I'm too excited to sit right now." She took her granddaughter's hand and said more somberly, "Thank you, Rhiann. Thank you for granting me this deep desire."

"I don't completely understand why at age eighty you want to even think about moving to a different state, but of course, Grams – if that is what you want, we'll do it." Rhiann smiled. "Besides, you know I enjoy exploring, and after living in West Yellowstone for that year, writing stories on Yellowstone Park and the surrounding area, I know how beautiful Montana is."

"I wish I had told you then how close you were to the homestead I grew up on – perhaps you could have gone there and seen it."

Rhiann wrinkled her brow. "Just how close was I?"

"Less than a two-hour drive."

"Oh, Grams! Why didn't you say anything? I would have gone!"

"I know, I know. Your grandpops wasn't welcomed into my family with open arms. That's a reason we rarely visited. So for that year you lived in West Yellowstone, I kept things to myself to not rock the boat and upset Grandpops. He wanted to put that all behind us, so I only saw my parents a few times during our marriage."

"Grams!"

The elderly woman nodded. "Things were different back then. In essence, I was disowned."

"You never told me that."

"No reason to. My parents died before you were born. My brother inherited that place and then sold it to someone else. That property hasn't been part of my family for the past forty-plus years."

"Then why? Why go back?"

"Because I have fond childhood memories. Oh, the work was hard, but it was a good life. I thought about going back after college, but I took the nursing job in Boise. A few months later, I met your grandfather. I had a new life ahead of me, and when you're twenty-something, even back then, you want to have your own life, away from prying eyes of family and small communities. At least some of us Irish lasses do."

Rhiann smiled at her grandmother and patted the older woman's hand. "And that's good for a time, but there's also a time to return to family."

"I'll have both if we can get property in Montana – my lovely granddaughter as family as well as my family of origin connection there plus a new adventure for the final chapter of my life."

Rhiann smiled and kissed her grandmother's cheek.

Tears glimmered in Grams' eyes. "Thank you for being so loyal and loving to your grandpops and me. I'll never be able to repay you for what you did for us ten years ago – giving up your life and future with Brandon, but I hope the inheritance I'll be able to leave you, the opportunity to start your own animal rescue sanctuary, will make it up in part."

Rhiann placed her hands on her grandmother's shoulder in a gentle manner. She peered into the woman's pale green eyes. "I've told you many times – you don't have anything to 'make up' for. When Erin and I needed you, you and Grandpops were there, and you helped us so much! That what family does. We are family, and we'll always be family. I'll go wherever you go and I'll always be with you."

Through misty eyes, her grandmother said, "I say, let's get this ball rolling!"

Rhiann grinned and raised a fist high into the air. "Look out, Montana! Here come the Kelly-McAllister women!"

Grams wrapped Rhiann in a warm, firm embrace.

"And who knows? There could be a Montana cowboy waiting just for you."

As she hugged her grandmother, she said, "Maybe so, Grams, but I might be better off finding a veterinarian if I'm going to run an animal rescue sanctuary!"

Rhiann and her beloved Grams shared a laugh.

DOES RHIANN FIND LOVE with a Montana cowboy or veterinarian? Find out in Book 1 of my Pet Rescue Romance series, titled *Rescue Road*!

Excerpt from Chapter 1 of ***Rescue Road***:

Rhiann Kelly twisted the lens on the digital camera, capturing the scene of two adult dogs sitting in front of a downed cottonwood tree. Golden leaves splayed on the ground, creating a natural carpet and accenting other autumn colors throughout the Montana campground. She smiled at the scene framed in the camera's viewfinder.

Rays of mid-morning sunlight danced among the aspens, cottonwoods, and pine trees and enveloped her canine subjects. As she took a deep breath to steady herself, Rhiann silently willed the wire-haired West Highland terrier and the coppery cocker spaniel to stay. Pressing the silver button atop the camera, she snapped two photos.

"Good dogs! Really good dogs!"

The four-footed creatures stood in union at her praise and wagged their tails. Rhiann walked to them and presented each with a soft treat from the pocket of her fleece jacket. First one and then the other nibbled the bacon-flavored morsel from her extended hand.

Rhiann repositioned the dogs to the right, closer to a russet-colored shrub. She coaxed the animals to sit and stay, and they obeyed. Rhiann walked back to the camera and glanced at the dogs. She smiled at the new scene. The animals' fur blended well with the colors of the serviceberry bush, its crimson branches and burnished leaves cascading toward heads of yellowing grasses.

"Stay!" Rhiann again commanded as she readjusted the tripod and camera. She looked through the viewfinder. *This will make a great adoption photo.*

Rhiann placed her index finger on top of the camera. Sticks snapped along the nearby wooded trail. Rhiann paused and raised her head. Her photo subjects looked to the left, and she glanced in that direction. Her green eyes widened.

Bear?

Leaving the camera and tripod, she swept the dogs into her arms and drew a deep breath. Knowing southwestern Montana provided prime habitat for such creatures and that October offered opportunity for food foraging before hibernation, she reprimanded herself under her breath.

"Why didn't I bring that bear spray?"

Leaves crunched as running steps padded closer. Rhiann sprinted toward the nearest concrete picnic table. The two dogs chorused a barking frenzy from the security of her embrace. Rhiann tried to hush them as she leaped upon the structure's seat and climbed to the higher tabletop. Twigs cracked as something rushed from the surrounding forest. She quivered and bit her lower lip to stifle a scream. She knew bears had poor eyesight, and if she kept quiet, perhaps the creature would move on without noticing her.

On impulse, her right hand delved into her jacket pocket in search of a defense weapon. However, the two wiggling dogs in her arms made the attempt difficult. Rhiann shushed them as her fingers closed around a set of keys. Her hand emerged from the pocket, and she whispered praise to the dogs plastered against her chest. Rhiann closed her eyes in silent prayer. The intruding noises ceased, and she re-opened her eyes. Her mouth rounded in an "O" when she saw what stared at her.

LEVI BUTLER GAWKED at the woman standing on top of the picnic table at Twin Bridges Campground—holding a pair of small dogs no less! The scene made him come to a complete stop after jogging the three-mile circular river trail and back to the parking lot. He muffled a smile and turned his head to squelch an eruption of laughter that rumbled in his chest.

Returning his gaze to the picnic table, he watched the dark-haired woman place a hand over her heart. The russet cocker spaniel jumped from her grasp. Instinct kicking in, Levi took a step forward, but the glower from the dog stopped him.

He heard the woman exhale. "Heavens! You scared me!"

"And you startled me," he replied.

"What are you doing here?" they asked simultaneously.

Levi chuckled. He reached a hand toward her and said, "Here, let me help you."

He noticed her hesitation, so he smiled. Dressed in black sweatpants and a long-sleeved dark blue T-shirt, he pointed to the emblem above his left pocket. Red lettering announced, "Jefferson County EMS."

"I promise—I'm one of the good guys."

Her eyes traveled to the insignia. The emerald spheres sparkled like jewels, catching him off-guard. Levi shook his head to banish any thought of attraction.

I need her to feel comfortable, not more frightened, he thought.

He maintained his smile and watched as she extended her arm. He clasped her hand and helped her to the ground.

"You ruined my shot," she said with a glare. "Who runs in a campground at 11 am on a Tuesday in October?"

He heard the frustration in her voice, tinged with a note of relief. "I'm sorry about scaring you," he said. "I go on duty in a few hours, so I needed to get my run in before work. Usually, during a weekday in autumn, no one is around."

"That's what I thought, too," she retorted.

She set the white terrier by her feet and reached up to the cocker spaniel. She helped the dog to the ground. She looked at Levi, and her face softened. "I admit, I'm glad you're not a bear."

He patted the can of spray on the belt at his hip. "That's why I have this."

Holding the dogs' leashes, the woman escorted them away from Levi. He noticed the camera and tripod.

"I take it you don't have bear spray?" Levi asked, taking a few steps closer.

She shrugged. "I planned on it but forgot it at home."

The woman pulled a biscuit from her jacket pocket and gave a piece to each dog. She walked closer to the camera, the small dogs trotting close behind her.

"Where's home?" Levi asked as he watched them.

The woman turned. Her eyes narrowed, and she frowned.

Levi shrugged. "I'm just curious. I've lived here for nearly fifteen years, and I don't believe I've seen you around."

"You likely haven't. I recently moved to the area."

"Oh? What brought you here?"

"Family. And these guys." She nodded toward the dogs.

He studied them a moment. "Nice-looking animals. Yours, I take it?"

"For now. The terrier is Molly, and the cocker is Max. They're available for adoption. The photos I'm taking will hopefully get them a new home."

"Do you work at the animal shelter near Bozeman?" Levi asked.

She shook her head. "I'm a pet rescue transport coordinator. I've visited Heart of the Valley Animal Shelter a couple of times during transports through the area. I'm setting up an animal sanctuary near Colter on land that's part of my family's heritage."

"Really? May I ask where?"

She hesitated and chewed her lower lip. Her emerald eyes gazed into his slate-colored ones. She glanced at the insignia on his shirt before responding. "A few miles west of town."

His eyebrows arched. "That's interesting. I live west of Colter, too. I don't recall seeing any for sale signs on properties around there lately."

"I bought the place for back taxes."

Levi remained silent a moment, his mind whirling with wonder as he pictured ranches in the area. He shook the cobwebs from his entangled thoughts and said, "Well, maybe we'll be neighbors. I'm intrigued by your idea of a rescue sanctuary. My future involves raising horses, and some will come from the Bureau of Land Management's wild horse adoption program."

Her face softened as she smiled. Levi immediately noticed her smooth complexion and high cheekbones.

"Sounds wonderful," she said. "I'd like to hear more about that sometime."

He returned her smile. "And I'd like to learn more about your sanctuary plans. Our area could use a strong rescue organization."

WHAT HAPPENS WHEN LEVI discovers Rhiann's ranch she purchased for back taxes was property he expected to inherit? And who's the man trying to take the land away from both of them? What about the dogs? Discover the answers to these questions and more when you buy your copy of *Rescue Road!*

Purchase ***Rescue Road*** on Amazon, Barnes and Noble, Kobo, and Apple Books!

Find on Amazon here:

https://amzn.to/2W7fpBe

Available in Kindle e-book and in print formats.

Find on the other e-book platforms here:

https://books2read.com/u/4DE9Oe

The book receives 4 and 5 star reviews!

WHAT SOME READERS SAY about *Rescue Road*:

Not only are deserved pups getting rescued in this story, but Rhiann and Levi, who have both been burned by love, get rescued and find new love. This book also has some suspense which keeps you guessing until the end about how it's going to turn out. If you like clean romance with a bit of suspense and cute pups needing homes, this is the book for you. – Mary B. – romance reader and author

What a clever idea for a sweet, clean romance. Bringing people together through rescue pets, second chances for both pets and people. – Linda C. – bookstore owner

Rescue Road is the first book in the Pet Romance Series and y'all, I loved every dang page of it! – Casey P. - author

Don't miss out!

Visit the website below and you can sign up to receive emails whenever GAYLE M. IRWIN publishes a new book. There's no charge and no obligation.

https://books2read.com/r/B-A-YLIJ-KLUJB

BOOKS 2 READ

Connecting independent readers to independent writers.

Also by GAYLE M. IRWIN

Pet Rescue Romance

Rescue Road

Finding Love at Compassion Ranch

Grams' Legacy

Rhiann's Rescue - A Holiday Prequel

About the Author

Gayle Irwin is an award-winning author and freelance writer. She is a contributor to seven *Chicken Soup for the Soul* books and the author of inspirational pet books for children and adults. She weaves important life lessons within her stories, including courage, kindness, perseverance, nature appreciation, and the importance of pet rescue and adoption. She volunteers for rescue organizations and donates a percentage of book sales to such groups. Her own pets are rescues that she and her husband adopted. Her first novel, *Rescue Road*, about a freelance writer turned animal rescue advocate who falls in love with a local EMT, published in November 2019 and is the first story in her Pet Rescue Romance series. Learn more about Gayle and her writing at www.gaylemirwinauthor.com.

Read more at https://gaylemirwinauthor.com/.